THE RAGGED BELIEVERS

Books by Robert Rayner

Colorland

The Atlantic Trilogy *series*
Defiant Island
The Ragged Believers

Coming Soon

Leaving Colorland
Flake

Second Wind
(An Atlantic Trilogy novel)

THE RAGGED BELIEVERS

Robert Rayner

SPEAKING VOLUMES, LLC
NAPLES, FLORIDA
2016

The Ragged Believers

ISBN 978-1-62815-327-9

For Beulah Caldwell, with thanks
for her advice on nursing in New Brunswick in the '30s.

Acknowledgments

Thanks to Elizabeth Margaris, for her endless support and encouragement, and Yvonne Wilson, for her prescience and persistence.

And thanks, always, to Nancy, for her honest and perceptive responses to drafts, and for her tolerance of the seclusion and incipient schizophrenia of writing.

Chapter One

On sunny afternoons in summer the girls in their white dresses lay on the rocks by the sea, as vacuous and unglamorous as the gulls wheeling above them, as serene and languorous as the seals on the further rocks. They talked of the men they had transported the night before, and joked, not unkindly, of their clients' foibles and confessions, their weaknesses and frantic lusts. Often I joined them, and they discussed my forlorn love for their colleague, Jenny, the prostitute who befriended me and lived with me, but denied me her love. They gossiped and drowsed the afternoons away, like sirens on the rocks, luring not sailors from the sea, but travellers from the highway across the meadow and beyond the Seashore Boarding House.

The highway then, in the late twenties, was no more than a potholed dirt road winding along the south coast of the province and through the forest between the gritty port city of Saint John and the ramshackle border town of St. Stephen. Travelling the eighty miles between the towns was an arduous journey and the boarding house was a convenient and pleasant overnight stopping point, offering accommodation and food, as well as the extra services of the girls.

"You wear white," Nurse told the girls, "because the boarding house is hospital, maternity home and abortion clinic, as well as hotel, dining room and brothel. And you are nurses, as well as chamber maids, cooks, waitresses and prostitutes."

Nurse was the founder of the Seashore Boarding House. She had decided always to wear white after her medical services were rejected by a hysterical woman because she did not look the part. She was changing sheets in the boarding house on a winter morning when she was called to one of the scattered communities that dotted the woods road between the towns. A frantic neighbour arrived and told her a woman in Messalonskee was drowning in baby's blood. Nurse abandoned the bed making and without changing out of her smock and headscarf accompanied the neighbour in his car. She found the woman lying in a pool of blood on the kitchen floor, surrounded by neighbours. The husband sobbed by the stove. Nurse knelt by the woman, who opened her eyes and grumbled at her, "I need a nurse, not a cleaning woman."

Nurse demanded a sheet, which the husband ripped from a bed, crying, "Our wedding sheets can be her shroud."

Nurse cut a hole in the centre of the sheet, dropped it over her head and tied it with a tea towel around her waist. She knelt beside her patient again, who opened her eyes and murmured to the white figure, "Thank you for coming, nurse. I think it's the baby."

The woman's pulse was barely perceptible, so Nurse placed a slab of kindling across two logs of wood and raised her patient's feet on it. She sent the husband to the brook to fetch ice, which she wrapped in a dishcloth and placed on the woman's abdomen. She sent a neighbour to Saint John to fetch the ambulance, while she stayed with the woman, renewing the ice and staunching the bleeding, until it arrived five hours later. As Nurse left, the husband said, "Thank you, nurse."

This was not the first time her nursing skill had been called upon by the woods communities, and it was her already established reputation which brought the neighbour seeking help, but after that she was always called Nurse, and always dressed as one.

"I might as well look the part," she said.

She wore a red sash with her uniform, and insisted the girls who later worked at the boarding house did too.

"It's red for the blood and danger of nursing," Nurse told them.

She would never admit that it betokened any other of the boarding house's services, although she decreed that when one of the girls was not wearing her red sash, it was her day off, from all her duties at the Seashore Boarding House.

I remember how charming that red sash at the girls' waists was as they walked from the boarding house to their cabins by the shore, the red and white figures becoming little more than a zigzag of bobbing red hyphens in the winter as their white dresses merged with the snow, in the summer blending red and white against the green of the meadow and the white and red of the daisies and Indian paint brush. I loved them all as sisters and friends, and Jenny as my all but wife, a wife who would not marry me, nor even love me, but who fulfilled that role as much as any man could wish. I used to have Jenny and crave her as a wife. Now I have neither wife nor Jenny, who dances in my memory like a child at a funeral.

Fire led me to Jenny, and to Nurse, and to the world of the Seashore Boarding House, with its ragged band of regulars, the commercial travellers, the mill workers, the loggers and truckers. I was a young lawyer then, and with offices in Saint John and St. Stephen often travelled the woods road between the towns. Halfway through one such trip I encountered a forest fire, which the fire crew from the nearby mill had almost under control. They waved me through the smoke but seconds later flames, fanned by a sudden breeze, erupted around me. I slowed, wondering whether to press on or turn back. As I looked at the flames licking through the brush on both sides of the road, I saw two signs pointing into the trees. I'd never noticed them before, despite often travelling that way. One stated simply, Nurse, and the other, Seashore Boarding House. At the same time as I saw the signs, Pastor Calvin Oagles appeared, mirage like, through the flames. He was walking out of the woods, his body wavering in the heat rising from the fires burning at the side of the road in front of him. He shouted at me, pointing in the air with one finger, "Lord's ire ignites the fire. Licentious games deserve the flames." I called to him to be careful but he ignored the warning, proclaiming, "When thou walkest through the fire, thou shalt not be burned; neither shall the fire kindle upon thee," and strode forward, inviolate, through the burning brush.

Charlie Kupkee, the fire crew boss, later told me Pastor Oagles's name. "Don't know he's genuine pastor, trained reverend," he said, sounding, as usual, like a garrulous telegram. "Doesn't dress himself like pastor, habiliate himself like reverend, but certainly acts like one, surely behaves such."

As suddenly as it had flared the fire died down and Pastor Calvin Oagles stood in the smoking brush by the road, now pointing through the trees in the direction indicated by the signs, chanting, "Lord's ire ignites the fire. Lust and desire feed the fire." I stopped the car beside him, thinking he needed help. He reached in and grabbed my arm, saying, "Some day she will burn with her sins. If she profane herself by playing the whore, she shall be burnt with fire."

He was immaculately dressed, all in black, except for a red handkerchief protruding neatly from the breast pocket of his jacket. He released me, nodded, and strode in the direction of Saint John, pointing his finger in the air again and crying, "Lord's ire ignites the fire. Either learn—or prepare to burn."

As I leaned out of the window to watch him disappear, a charred branch fell against the car and gashed the corner of my eye. While I was still holding my head in pain, the mill fire crew arrived and helped me into their truck, which I felt turn off the road in the direction shown by the signs.

Charlie said, "Need treatment, require first aid. Transport you to clinic, take you to Nurse."

The Board of St. Michael's Hospital, Saint John
- MEMO -

DATE: 22ⁿᵈ April 1916
TO: Nurse Melody Medley
FROM: G. Wilburton, Secretary to the Board

You will be aware that your unfortunate liaison with one of our hospital physicians has been the cause of some concern to the Hospital Board, as well as being the topic of much undesirable speculation among the staff.

Please appear before the Board at their next meeting, April 30ᵗʰ 1916, at 2 p.m., in the Board Room, to discuss this matter.

With blood seeping into my eyes and my hand clamped across them, I had no idea of my surroundings or my rescuers, only of a short ride, of a bend in the track, and of being led up some steps into what seemed a fairly spacious room. Our footsteps echoed on a bare wooden floor whose unevenness I could feel even through my shoes. The room smelled of damp wood and beeswax and warm leather, all of which mingled with the low tide smell from outside. I heard one of the fire crew ask for Nurse, and a woman's voice answered that Nurse was busy curing Gerry Baxter's girl, adding, "Sit him in here. I'll tend to him." I was placed in a chair. A hand clapped me on the shoulder and someone said, "You'll be all right now," and before I could even thank them the men had gone, their footsteps echoing again across the room and clattering on the steps outside. For a minute or two I sat alone, dazed by the injury and intrigued by my surroundings. I was still bewildered by the venom directed by a man of God (so I took the man in the woods to be) at someone here in the benign profession of nurse and at an establishment as innocuous as a boarding house. Then footsteps approached, lighter than those of the men, and my hands were lifted from my eyes. I heard, "I'm Jenny. Let me look," and as I blinked away blood all I could see in front of me was the white of a dress and a red sash across it. I closed my eyes again and while she bathed and bandaged the wound, she told me that I was in the Seashore Boarding House.

"And you work here?"

"Yes."

"You work as a nurse—in a boarding house."

"Yes. You can open your eyes now."

She stepped back. She was barely out of her teens, with hair the colour of cattails in winter, and a body as provocative as a puppy's, inviting touch, promising a teasing repulse, or wanton, luxurious submission.

Jenny looked carefully and thoughtfully at me, frowning a little and tilting her head to one side. "Sometimes I work as a nurse. Mostly I help with the running of the boarding house. Have you never heard of the Seashore Boarding House?"

Her voice was husky, with the rising lilt peculiar to the province.

"Should I have heard of it?"

"You must move in very limited social circles."

This was said ironically and smiling but I blushed at its unwitting truth. It wasn't that I moved in limited social circles; I moved in no social circles at all. I had tried to be sociable as I established my practice but I found the world of business relationships and obligations pervasive and shallow and perverted and, when I rejected that social world, I became suspect, a successful businessman but single, lacking the solidity and respectability a wife and family would bestow. Then, as my social alienation grew, so did my emotional isolation, and while I longed ingenuously for romance and love, their prospect receded.

I managed to say, still blushing, "I confess I do."

"Perhaps we can do something about that."

She smiled down at me and as she worked on the dressing on my eye, her fingertips wandered briefly and caressingly to each side of my face.

There was an urgent call of "Jenny" from upstairs and I was left alone. I was in what seemed to be a dining room. A dozen rough wooden tables, round, thick and sturdy, were spaced around the room and a few deep arm chairs covered in worn leather were pushed against the walls. Behind a small reception counter at the back of the room, a flight of stairs rose and turned abruptly. The setting reminded me of a saloon in a western movie, awaiting boisterous, lawless revelry. The floor, as I guessed when I was brought in, consisted of bare pine boards, wide and unevenly worn, so that the surface was smooth but undulating. The walls, more wide pine boards, were bare. All that saved the room from austerity were jars of wild flowers—lupines, pink and purple and blue—on the tables and the warm glow accorded the wood by the afternoon sun shining through the windows which looked out across the veranda to the meadow and the sea. I rose and crossed to the windows. My car was parked at the end of the track through the woods by which I had arrived. One of the fire crew must have driven it in and left it for me. I'd forgotten all about it. I looked back at the empty room and the stairs. I could hear voices but still my nurse did not reappear. I opened the door and ventured quietly out onto the veranda. At that moment a woman somewhere in the boarding house began to sob loudly and, feeling I was intruding, I descended the veranda steps and set off across the meadow which lay between the house and the rocky shore. Pocomoonshine Bay, with trees crowding down to its deserted beaches, stretched away on one side and on the other swept inwards, forming a cove protected by an outcrop of rocks. The tide was low and the salt smell of the sea mingled with the fecund odour of rotting seaweed. Among the green sheen of seaweed on the furthest rock, which became an island as each wave surged around it, the sleek bodies of dozens of seals basked. Further in, the girls lay, in their white dresses, like injured gulls with wings outstretched.

The path forked halfway across the meadow, leading on one side to the beach, on the other to three small cabins nestling where the meadow met the rocks at the end of the cove. I followed the trail down to the beach, where one of the languid figures on the rocks, hearing my steps, sat up and stretched. In slow motion, seaweed in a gentle current, the other followed as she, too, became aware of my presence. They eyed me, warily but invitingly, one dark figure and one fair, draped sensuously on the rocks.

"Who do you want?" said one. This was Colleen, I learned later. Her black hair fell in a mass around her narrow shoulders. She was as tall and rangy as her companion was short and big boned.

"I was just looking around. I hope you don't mind."

"'Course not, honey," said the other, Megan, who, when she stood, came to Colleen's shoulder, and whose blonde hair was cut into a square bob. She stretched again and adjusted the red sash around her waist.

"Are you a musician man?" Colleen asked.

Before I could say that I was not and to ask why she wanted to know, Megan interrupted with, "Take no notice of her foolishness."

"I'm on the lookout for a musician man," Colleen went on, unabashed. "There's something about a musician man that's so … enticing." She looked at me from the corner of her eye and winked before continuing, "But never mind if you're not. Look us over at your leisure; choose the one to give you pleasure."

As she spoke, Colleen put her hands on her hips below her red sash and slid them down her thighs, pulling her dress tightly against her body. They both laughed.

I blushed again and stammered, "Do you mind if I sit with you? I'm waiting for Jenny. She was looking after me and was called away."

I sat down and the girls immediately and flatteringly sat themselves on each side of me. They smelled of the sea, enticing and fresh.

Megan, leaning so close to me that her hair brushed my face, said, "Tell me, honey. Is this your first visit to the Seashore Boarding House?"

I explained how I came to be there, concluding, "And do you work here with Jenny?"

Jenny herself answered. "They are my colleagues and my friends."

She was standing behind us at the edge of the meadow and as I looked around the breeze from the sea swirled her hair off her shoulders into a halo backlit by the sun and pressed her white dress against her legs. She stepped lightly across the rocks and, offering her hand to help me stand, said, "Come with me. I have to finish dressing your wound."

I stood and found myself looking down at her, her face level with my neck, so that later, the first time we embraced, she said, "How well we fit together," lightly and playfully. I took it as a portent of love and replied, "Fit to love each other, too," and when her face clouded and she turned away, realized I had made some mistake. Her face always revealed both her character and her mood, her shifting warmth and severity. In profile, as she turned away that time, she was all strong angles, sharp and uncompromising, her chin receding suddenly, her nose shaped to a sudden, unexpected point, her brow arching abruptly backwards. But as she turned back, face on, forgiving, those angular features softened into an ephemeral, delicate beauty.

We walked back across the meadow to the boarding house. It stood square and symmetrical, with four shuttered windows, and the door and the veranda steps at the centre. Its wide clapboards, weather-blasted to grey, formed a textural counterpoint to the tuckamore on the edge of the beach, and its glinting tin roof imitated the sparkle of the sea. On the veranda, which tilted towards one end where the supports were rotting and giving way, another white dressed and red sashed figure stood, this one older, perhaps in her late thirties, some twenty years older than the girls.

"This is Nurse," said Jenny.

I looked up at a fine boned face whose striking beauty was heightened rather than diminished by maturity. Auburn hair framed the lines of age and weariness and weather wear which coursed from her wide brown eyes and across her tanned face. She descended the steps and approached us, holding her hand out to me. As she moved to greet me, it was with such natural grace and elegance, and with her head held so high and proudly, that I thought her exceptionally tall until, when she was close to me, I realized she stood less than my average height. Her hand in mine felt rough and worn but as I released it, I noticed how delicate it was nevertheless in shape and size.

Nurse said to Jenny, "Miss Baxter is resting. She'll be all right now," and to me, "Welcome to the Seashore Boarding House. Let me take a look at your dressing."

"It's as well cleaned and bandaged as if I'd been to the hospital," I said. "And I'm grateful to the boarding house and to you and Jenny for taking care of me. It's a surprise to find such care in the middle of the woods—in a boarding house."

"We surprise a lot of people," Nurse said, with a mischievous smile which briefly softened the tiredness of her face. She added, "Jenny, I have to rest for a while. Will you deal with any visitors?"

As she spoke I became more aware of the tiredness clouding her face, not a temporary tiredness this but a long, deep-seated weariness, and a fragment of a song popular at the time came, unbidden, to my mind: *Woman's life is care and duty, faded looks and ravaged beauty.*

At the door of the dining room she turned to tell me, "We will be serving supper shortly. I hope you can stay." Then slowly, wearily, she went inside.

Jenny bit her lip and shook her head. "She's so tired. She barely slept again last night. She delivered a girl to Mrs. Feltham over in Poccassee. Then she found old Mr. Kinney waiting for her outside—at two in the morning! He said he'd seen her over at the Felthams's and wanted Nurse to check on his wife. She was having trouble breathing again. It was after four when Nurse got back here and then she had to be up at seven to deal with Miss Baxter."

"And now she's going to serve supper?" I asked.

"No. We'll do that tonight, Megan, Colleen and me. Are you going to stay?"

"Of course."

"I'll make you tea while you wait."

We walked across the meadow again, this time taking the path to the cabins. Colleen and Megan, still lying on the rocks, waved lazily as we passed. Jenny led me inside the cabin which, as my eyes grew accustomed to the dark, I saw was as plain as the exterior, consisting simply of a kitchen, with a stove, a table, and two chairs, and a bedroom beyond. I could see Jenny's bed, dishevelled, through an open door. As she moved about preparing tea, I sat at the kitchen table and admired again her lightness and grace. When she placed my tea before me, she said, taking my head in her hands again and standing close, "Let me see that wound once more." Her sea scent, the same as I smelled on the girls on the rocks, filled my head and I felt myself growing dizzy.

The sound of pots banging together, and the voices of Megan and Colleen calling that it was time to go up to the house to prepare supper, brought me back to reality.

"That's the Bear Pots," explained Jenny, seeing my surprise. "We use them to call guests to supper."

"The Bear Pots?"

"That's a Nurse story. You'll probably hear it at supper. The guys like to tell it to newcomers." She adjusted her red sash, watching me, and said, "I have to prepare supper. You stay here and finish your tea. Come up to the house when you're ready."

By the time I finished my tea and followed Jenny up to the dining room, the few tables were full. I hung back at the top of the veranda steps, seeing the crowded dining room. My habitual social caution—instinctive or learned; I don't know which—warned me to flee the Seashore Boarding House now. It cautioned against the easy relationships and friendships I sensed there, which I hesitated to trust because they seemed to demand nothing in return. I didn't know how to respond to the ready kindness of the men in the fire crew and the girls on the rocks. Moreover, the sensuousness and flirtatiousness of the girls unnerved me. I was disturbed by the incipient violence of the raving man of God and the curious protectiveness I felt already toward the objects of his rage and invective. It would be easy to depart now, quietly. I could leave a little money somewhere as a token of thanks and go, with no risk taken and no obligation placed upon me. All I had to do was turn around, step quietly down into the growing darkness, climb into my car, and drive back to the city.

I turned.

The door opened and Jenny said, "Don't be shy. Come on in. I'll introduce you."

I looked back. She held out her hand. I took it and she led me in. Among the men in the dining room I discovered Charlie—I could tell him by his voice—and some others who had helped me at the fire, who nodded as I entered.

Charlie waved me over, calling, "Join us. Congregate with us."

Jenny sat me at his table, said, "This is Duncan Strathearn, the patient you brought to us from the fire," and went to the kitchen.

"This Lamarre. Lamarre Fontaine," Charlie said, indicating the young man sitting beside him.

Lamarre Fontaine nodded and supplied, "From Eagle Rock. From up north originally. Lameque. Lamarre from Lameque. That's me."

His dark complexion complemented his black hair, a shock of which fell across his forehead.

Charlie went on, "This Sonny. Sonny Cline," gesturing toward an older man sitting across the table.

Sonny Cline also nodded. "From Ratters Lake, nearest community to the boarding house, a couple of miles through the woods from here. Lived there all my life, all forty years of it, working in the woods."

His weathered face and brawny build echoed his words.

Charlie concluded, "And this Missus. Mrs. Charlie." He put his arm around the woman sitting beside him, the only woman in the dining room apart from the girls. Mrs. Charlie looked up and smiled. Her hair was as grey as Charlie's but her complexion, unlike her husband's, was a vibrant pink. I caught a glimpse of a round face with shining eyes and cheeks dimpled by her smile before she looked quickly down again.

Charlie, Sonny and Lamarre looked at me. I wondered how I was supposed to respond to the introductions. Was I supposed to reveal something of myself in return? And how much of myself?

I stalled with, "I'm grateful for your help in the fire today."

"Nothing, nought," Charlie said, at the same time as Lamarre muttered, "De rien," and Sonny, "Forget it."

They still looked at me. Mrs. Charlie glanced up at me, too.

12

"Duncan Strathearn," I offered, looking around the table, forgetting that Jenny had already introduced me.

"From?" Sonny prompted.

"Saint John."

"City man," Lamarre put in.

"Born and bred," I said, wondering if this somehow counted against me.

"On road a lot? Travel much?" Charlie asked.

"Not much. I have an office in Saint John and another in St. Stephen, so I'm often driving between them. But that's about all my travelling."

"Office? What sort of office?" Lamarre asked.

"Law. I'm a lawyer."

There was a pause and I wondered again whether the information I offered counted against me in some way.

Sonny asked, "Good money, is it?"

"Enough." In all my social introductions and exchanges in the city, I'd never been asked this. "Enough," I said again. "The money's not bad, but …" I would probably have ignored such a question in the city, in the unlikely event of its being asked. If I had chosen to answer, my response certainly would have been terse. Here, however, I went on, "But …" They continued to gaze at me, even Mrs. Charlie. "But that's not why I do it, the law."

"Why then?" Sonny demanded.

"Because it's good to feel you're helping people. That's why you do it. You have to charge, of course. You have to make a living. But really you do the job to help people in trouble. At least, that's what I think."

I looked around at them. I hadn't intended to speak so much, or so openly, about myself and my work. I added, "That's what I believe, anyway."

Sonny grinned. Lamarre nodded. Mrs. Charlie dimpled.

Charlie said, "Help, yes. Assist, right. Beliefs good. Convictions worthy."

Charlie and Mrs. Charlie went to talk across the room and while they were gone from our table Sonny confided, "You'll get used to Charlie's way of talking. It's because of all those years working in the granite sheds. It was making him deaf, so he came to work in the woods, looking for peacefulness. But it was too late. His hearing was as good as gone by then. It was so noisy in the sheds he got in the habit of making everything he said as short as he could. Then, when it was peaceful in the woods, he liked it so much he just wanted to talk. So now he shortens everything he says, out of habit, then says it over. Just as well Mrs. Charlie doesn't say much. She'd never get a word in."

"How much does he hear? And understand?"

"Hears little. Understands everything. He lip reads. Taught himself."

Charlie and Mrs. Charlie rejoined us. Charlie's hair was a shaggy grey mat, his eyebrows stood up like grey fins, and even his skin was grey. It was as if his whole body had absorbed the dust of the granite he had worked with in his youth.

I asked my dinner companions about the boarding house, commenting on how successful a business it seemed to be. "There are three ladies employed here, as well as Nurse herself," I offered.

Charlie smiled, and Sonny and Lamarre chuckled and nodded as I spoke of the ladies employed there. All the girls were kept very busy, Charlie said, and added, "But, though, was time, period, few years, Nurse alone, by herself, helping anyone miles around couldn't reach doctor."

"Don't the doctors in the city mind people coming to her for medical help?" I asked.

"They send cases to her, direct patients her way," said Charlie. "Long journey here for physician, lengthy ride out for doctor. Grateful to her helping out, thankful for assisting. Doctors busy enough, overworked sufficiently. Her too. Always busy. Always treating, curing. Doesn't rest, never stops."

As if to confirm Charlie's words, at that moment a horse drawn wagon careened to a halt before the veranda. A woman leapt from the wagon, ran up the stairs, and burst into the dining room. The man with her climbed down more slowly, cradling in his arms a tiny girl, who lay unmoving.

Before the woman could speak, Sonny was on his feet, calling, "Nurse—quick", as he ran outside. Jenny echoed him, shouting up the stairs behind the reception counter, "Nurse, come quick." The man was standing at the foot of the veranda steps, holding the little girl before him, as if offering her to the Seashore Boarding House. Tears poured down his face as he moaned, "My child, my Brandy, she's dead. We've lost her. I know it. She's dead, Nurse, isn't she?"

Sonny shook off his jacket and tucked it around the child as the father still held her. Nurse flew downstairs, through the dining room and down the steps. The diners followed, spreading out along the veranda as they spilled through the door. Lamarre was beside me and said quietly, "Just watch Nurse now. See why we love her so."

"Mr. Turner, isn't it? From Poccassee," Nurse asked the man.

The father nodded. "And here's Brandy. Brandy who you delivered three years ago. And now she's dead."

The mother, supported by the girls, wept and prayed among us on the veranda. "Blessed are those who mourn, husband, for they shall be comforted."

"Be strong and of good courage, do not fear, nor be afraid," the man responded.

"What happened to Brandy?" Nurse asked, her fingers searching around the child's wrist.

"For the Lord your God, He is the one who goes with you. He will not leave you, nor forsake you," the mother wailed.

Sonny shook the father by the shoulder and repeated, "Brandy. What happened to her?"

"My flesh and my heart fail; but God is the strength of my heart," the mother mourned.

"The strength of my heart," the father echoed. He added, to Nurse and Sonny, "Lightning strike. Lightning hit her. She was playing in the yard, in the mud and the rain. Then—a lightning storm, no warning. Mother went out to bring the child in and before she reached her, the lightning hit her. And Brandy was lying there, in the mud, and the rain still falling. We grabbed her up. Brought her here. And we've lost our Brandy."

"Be strong and of good courage," the mother called again.

"God is our refuge and our strength, and a very present help in times of trouble," the father responded.

"Bring Brandy," Nurse told Mr. Turner. "Follow me."

"Therefore we will not fear," the mother mourned and the father, swaying with his eyes closed, joined her in chorus, "Though the earth be removed and though the mountains be carried into the midst of the sea."

"Sonny, you'll have to do it. Take the child," Nurse commanded.

Sonny scooped the lifeless body from the father, bundling his jacket tightly around her. "Do what? What shall I do with the poor mite?"

"Drop her in the rain barrel," Nurse said quietly.

Sonny's eyes widened. He shook his head and whispered, "Nurse, I can't do that."

"Sonny—the rain barrel. Drop her in it," Nurse insisted.

The mother and father were on their knees, the father before the veranda where Nurse and Sonny stood with the little girl, the mother falling between Megan and Colleen. The parents prayed together: "This is my comfort in my affliction, for Your Word has given me life. God is our refuge and our strength."

Sonny climbed the steps and strode through us to the rain barrel that stood at the end of the veranda. He looked back once, questioningly, at

Nurse. She nodded firmly and he dropped the child in. The parents, realizing what was happening, screamed in unison, at the same time as a desperate wail sounded from the rain barrel.

Nurse, who had followed Sonny, said, "Lift her out and give her to me."

Sonny placed the dripping, shrieking child in Nurse's arms. She comforted the child, gave her a quick examination, and handed her on to the parents, who had abandoned their prayers and hurried after Sonny and Nurse.

"It's a miracle," said the father. "Praise the Lord and bless you, Nurse."

"She was deeply unconscious, not dead," Nurse explained. "The shock of the cold water brought her round, that's all. She seems to be recovered but bring her back here tomorrow and I'll take another look at her. Take her home now. Let her sleep."

The mother climbed onto the wagon and the father set Brandy carefully into her arms. He shook Sonny's hand, embraced Nurse, said, "Bless you," again, and climbed up beside the mother. They turned the wagon and set off on the track to the road. The diners watched them disappear, then turned back into the boarding house, the girls leading the way and disappearing into the kitchen.

"See what I mean?" Lamarre said, as we sat at the table. "That's why we love Nurse."

"Where did she learn her medicine?"

Lamarre shrugged. Mrs. Charlie smiled. Charlie said vaguely, "Long story. Lengthy tale, history. Don't know all ins, outs, of it. Ignorant of details."

Sonny rejoined us, shaking his head. "I believe Nurse when she says the lass was just unconscious. But when I took her from the father, I couldn't see any sign of life. I thought she was gone."

Nurse was last to come in. As she entered, the diners broke into applause. She held up her hands and shook her head, as if to dismiss the congratulations. She crossed to our table and said to Sonny, "Thank you for your help."

"I thought you were crazy, telling me to drop the girl in the rain barrel. I should have known better."

"It's an old trick, shocking lightning victims with cold water. I learned it from old Mrs. Hooper at Eagle's Rock." She turned to me. "Mr. Strathearn, Jenny tells me you are a lawyer. May I talk with you for a moment?"

As I followed her across the room I said, "The girls told me you were resting. Is your rest often disturbed by medical emergencies like this?"

"Yes—but I don't mind. I find it hard to rest and to sleep and a diversion is almost welcome," she answered over her shoulder.

She led me behind the counter—her office, she said—and asked me a straightforward question concerning a property tax assessment the boarding house had received. I dealt easily with her concern and she thanked me for my help, offering to pay for my legal services. Of course I refused, saying that, on the contrary, I had been wondering how much I owed for their first aid, not to mention the supper.

"You owe nothing for the first aid, unless you want to make a donation to the boarding house to go toward providing medicines and bandages and so on," Nurse said. "That's all we ever ask. And as for the supper, let's wait until you leave."

As I turned back to the dining room, I noticed, set on a shelf below the counter, hidden from view except from behind it, a faded photograph in a stained gilt frame. For a moment, glancing at it, I thought it was a portrait of some film actress. Then I looked again, more carefully. The woman in the photograph, caught in soft focus half profile, had cheek bones so delicately sculpted they threw a pool of shadow between her eyes and mouth. She gazed dreamily past the camera into the distance with eyes wide and beguiling. Her lips were pushed forward in a gentle, provocative pout which, with the slight snub of her nose, turned her face from austere beauty to earthy, waif like sensuousness. I glanced from the photograph to Nurse and back. Her cheeks were gaunt now, rather than finely shadowed, her eyes tired rather than seductive. With the texture of her skin coarsened by age and rough weather in the woods, she was society beauty turned feral, but still arrestingly attractive.

Seeing my glance, Nurse blushed and said, "My vanity. I should destroy it. It was my graduation day. I was a nurse, at last."

I returned to my table, leaving Nurse behind the counter, sitting and gazing wistfully, it seemed, at the photograph.

St. Michael's Hospital, 123-125 Waterloo Road, Saint John, New Brunswick
23rd April 1916

Dear Mr. Wilburton,
I tender my resignation herewith as nurse at St. Michael's Hospital, effective from this date.
I thank the Hospital Board for giving me the opportunity of both training and serving at St. Michael's.
Respectfully Yours—Melody Medley, R.N.

The door burst open and an enormous man, dressed in a dark suit, entered with, "Greetings, m'darlings." His black, lustrous hair hung over his shoulders and his belly over his belt. He was followed by a frail, older man, dressed in a morning suit, who swept off his homburg with a flourish, saying, "Nurse, Mrs. Charlie, girls, sirs, good evening." They looked around, saw me, and marched to our table, the first of them patting Megan on the rear as she passed with a plate of food.

The giant boomed, extending his hand to me, "Randy Fudge, traveller in sanitation, meeting your bodily needs with taste and economy. Welcome to the Seashore Boarding House."

His companion added quietly, also offering his hand, "Sir, I am the Count. Count Yanovsky. I travel in women's underwear." He paused, chuckled, and added, "I mean, I travel and sell ladies' underwear, and other garments. I'm delighted to make your acquaintance."

I rose and shook their hands. Randy Fudge's grip was crushing, the Count's gentle. I was about to introduce myself, wondering again how much the social conventions of the boarding house obliged me to reveal, when Sonny said for me, "He's Duncan Strathearn, from Saint John. A lawyer. Been a patient here today, with a head injury from the fire. We hope he'll be back, now he's found us."

The newcomers joined the table.

Randy said to me, "So, m'darling, you are a peddler, like the Count and me. We peddle our merchandise and you peddle the law." He announced to the table, "The law's an honourable and a proud profession."

"He's proud of it," Lamarre said.

"The way he does it, it's honourable and proud," Sonny asserted.

"Thank you," I said.

"Where do you practice?" the Count asked.

"Saint John and St. Stephen. And you—where do you sell?"

"My large colleague and I travel throughout the south of the province. We sell to the shops in the towns and cities, and in the rural areas to households."

"We cover lots of ground in our business, eh, Count, m'darling?" Randy put in. "We must have travelled thousands of miles over the years. Mind you, it's not as hard as it used to be, now that we've got the motorised transportation."

He waved toward the window, through which I could see a large van. "Come, m' darling. I'll give you a glimpse of the bathroom of the future."

He grasped my arm, almost lifting me out of my chair, and we went outside. Randy Fudge's van had *Worley Washes the World* emblazoned on its side. He opened the rear with a flourish, revealing a complete bathroom set, tub, washbasin and toilet. The floor and sides of the van were tiled so that it resembled a miniature bathroom.

"Mr. Worley makes the best," he assured me. "It's the most modern there is. Attractive and …" He leaned forward, confidentially. "Hygienic as all hell."

Nurse later showed me the comment Randy had written in the guest book after his first visit: "Thanks for a fine meal and lodging. Will recommend it to fellow travellers. Particularly enjoyed the experience of the outhouse. Like crapping in a museum."

"Your friend travels in style," I said, admiring the Count's automobile, parked behind the van. It was a huge Hudson wagon, with wood paneled sides, the back loaded with boxes.

"A nice vehicle, but the Count struggles with it, don't you, m'darling?"

Randy turned to the Count, who had followed us out, and now stood above us on the veranda, his hands clasped behind him. The Count turned his gaze from the meadow and the sea to the Hudson. He nodded and confirmed, "I struggle with the confounded contraption."

"How do you mean—struggle?"

"I've been driving it for only six months…"

Randy interrupted, "He didn't want to drive, you know. He only got the Hudson because his employers …"

"That'd be Simpson's Lingerie and Styles, out of Halifax," the Count put in.

"… His employers told him he had to give up the old post chaise because a horse couldn't get him around his sales route quick enough. Isn't that right, Count?"

"That's quite correct. And in those six months—six short months—I've had to learn not only how to start the machine, but how to steer, and to change the gears, and to work my feet on the pedals. It's a complex operation, as you'll be aware. And now, as if that's not enough, I've got the new railway line on the other side of St. Stephen to deal with."

Randy interrupted again. "He doesn't understand the railroad crossings."

"I understand them perfectly well," the Count insisted. "They are designed to carry the automobile safely over the tracks."

"Tell him what you do when you get to the railroad crossing, then."

The Count pursed his lips and shook his head at his friend, who demanded, "Go on. Tell him."

The Count turned back to me. "I blow my horn to warn the trains I'm coming across the tracks."

"And over he goes, without stopping. I keep telling him he's supposed to wait and look, but straight over he goes."

"It is not my responsibility to worry about the passage of the trains. It is the job of any new fangled means of transportation to be aware of, and to grant precedence to, existing modes of travel. The automobile was here before the train, and therefore takes precedence, just as the horse takes precedence over the automobile."

I smiled at the exchange, as Randy shook his head, laughing affectionately at his friend. "Poor old Count, you nearly gave up the job when you had to give up your horse, eh, m'darling?"

"Perhaps I should have done."

"Never. Not you."

The Count explained to me, "I confess I thought of giving up the business when I was told that the horse and carriage was no longer a viable means of merchandising. And, indeed, I could have retired years ago, anyway, but I decided then I'd miss the life too much, and came to the same decision when I contemplated life without the travel, even if that meant travel by automobile and not by horse and wagon. You understand, we travellers end up with no home except the road, and no friends except those we meet on the road. Just as we have met you, my new friend."

The Count gave a little, formal bow in my direction. I'd been moved by their ready acceptance of me, a stranger at the Seashore Boarding

House, and by the confidences they shared about their life on the road. I was accustomed to the distant relationships of my business world. Now I was moved anew by the Count's naming me a friend, although it was done lightly and casually.

Randy elaborated, "There's always a welcome here from Nurse, and then there's the girls, and the bed and breakfasts, and the suppers. The Seashore Boarding House is a fine place for those of us on the road, eh, Count? And it's Nurse that's made it such a going institution. Mind you, m'darling ..." He held up a huge warning finger. "It wasn't always like this. It was a struggle for her when she first opened."

From the Desk of Dr. Noel Gallant
173a Manawagonish Terrace, Saint John, New Brunswick
24ᵗʰ April 1916

Dear Melody,

I know it would be impolitic for us to meet under the present circumstances, so I am here at the hospital early, leaving this note in your mailbox in the hope that this will enable us secret communication.

I have a plan! I have an old house—a former boarding house—in the woods between Saint John and St. Stephen. It was left to me by a distant relative, years ago, and I have never used it. I would like to sign the deeds over to you, so that it might afford you an income, now that your nursing career seems to be over (mea culpa), as well as afford us a secret rendezvous, away from the city. What do you think of my plan?

Your—Noel

Randy led the way back inside, where we rejoined Mr. and Mrs. Charlie, and Lamarre and Sonny, as the girls served supper. Lamarre overheard Randy's comment on the hard early days of the Seashore Boarding House and recalled, shaking his head, "How she struggled when she first opened, before the mill was built."

"Don't know how managed financially, made ends meet, before mill," Charlie added.

"But it's been booming since then, with all the loggers and truckers and mill workers coming here looking for lodging and food and ... relaxation," Sonny enthused.

"And when the woods communities grew more prosperous, that brought the Count and me along," Randy told me. Megan leaned across the table as she served and Randy patted her rump again as he went on, "And I'm pleased to say it brought these young ladies along, too, to live in their cabins down by the shore and to help Nurse out with the boarders and the bed and breakfasts and with serving the suppers." He concluded, expansively, sitting back in his chair and opening his arms to indicate the whole room, "Whenever we hear the Bear Pots, we know it means a good meal, in good company, served by these fine young ladies."

"The Bear Pots!" I said, remembering how we had been summoned to supper. "Jenny said I'd hear the story of the Bear Pots."

"That's a Nurse story we often tell to newcomers," said Lamarre.

Melody was alone at the Seashore Boarding House. She had spent a week cleaning and repairing the old house, its dining room and kitchen downstairs, the six bedrooms upstairs. It had stood empty for many years and now it was ready to resume its function as a boarding house. After living on sandwiches all week, she cooked her first meal on the newly cleaned wood stove.

She carried her supper outside in order to enjoy the last of the evening sun as she ate. She sat on the veranda and a bear walked out of the woods across the meadow, making for the source of the food smell that had attracted it. She dropped her plate, bolted back into the house, and slammed the door. Through the window she watched the animal mount the veranda and devour the food. Then it raised its snout. She realized it was still seeking the source of the smell—the still warm pots in the kitchen behind her. She ran into the kitchen. Grabbed the pots, intending to throw them out of the window, hoping that would satisfy its hunger and curiosity. But before she could return she heard the animal rip off the screen door. Heard the rake of claws against the inner door. She reached the window, almost sick with fear, and heaved it upwards. At the same time the door crashed inwards, swinging from one hinge. The bear shouldered past it and made for the strong smell it sensed close by. Terrified, she released the window. It dropped with a crash of breaking glass. The bear stopped, startled. With sudden inspiration, she continued and augmented the noise, banging the pots together. The bear retreated a step. She screamed, a long drawn out ululation at the highest pitch she could reach. Her mouth was wide and revealed (so she fancied) teeth as ready to rip and devour as the bear's. It retreated another step. Its rear end backed through the door. She stepped forward, still beating the pots together.

As loud as she could she shouted anything that came into her head: "This is the Seashore Boarding House you big bugger bear and this is my home and my supper and not for you so take a hike back into the woods you bastard bear."

It turned and ran, down the steps and across the meadow, looking back just once—sheepishly, she thought—before disappearing into the trees. She pursued it as far as the bottom of the steps, calling after it, "And if you want another scare try coming round here again big bloody bugger bear."

Then she collapsed on the steps, terrified and exultant, shivering, astonished at the silence which closed in on her invective and her clamour.

Lamarre concluded: "After that she felt sorry for the bear, and started leaving it scraps of food, but at the edge of the woods, not close to the house."

"And she hung the pots outside, like a warning to it not to come too close, and they've been there ever since those early days," Sonny added.

Randy said, "You'll hear plenty of Nurse stories, m'darling, if you become a regular at the Seashore Boarding House. Some of them change a bit in the telling, but they were all true to start with."

They all laughed. Then Charlie grew serious. "Nurse saint to people round here, angel to folk in these parts. Don't ever say word against her, never utter phrase criticizing her. Folk attack you, people tear you apart."

25

"I met someone in the woods—a churchman, I think, although I don't know of what denomination—who seemed opposed to her, and to the boarding house."

"Pastor Calvin Oagles, that'd be, sounds like," said Charlie, his grey eyebrows moving together as he frowned. The others nodded grimly. Across the dining room the girls paused in their serving and clearing of tables, and heads turned toward us as conversation halted around the room.

Randy added, "He has a church in Saint John, a kind of church, and he sees himself as some sort of saviour of the world. And that includes saving us."

"Saving us from who?"

"From Nurse and the girls, I guess."

There was a beat of silence in the room before the girls resumed their work and the diners their conversations. Charlie asked whether I was staying the night. "Ask Jenny whether do bed, breakfast," he suggested, with a wink. Then, "Home, missus," he said, and he and Mrs. Charlie left.

I was still puzzling over the remark about bed and breakfast when Nurse approached me again and also asked whether I'd like to stay for the night. I considered the remaining distance of my journey and the late hour, and the thought of seeing more of Jenny, and decided to stay.

"If you'd like bed and breakfast, we'll be pleased to oblige," she offered.

I declined, explaining that I would have to leave very early and that I would get breakfast in St. Stephen.

Nurse looked thoughtfully at me and said, "Jenny will show you to your room when you're ready." She went upstairs.

Jenny, Megan and Colleen reappeared, kitchen and dining room chores apparently complete. As Jenny went around the room lighting the lamps, the Count said, "How about a song, Lamarre?" From an inside pocket

Lamarre produced a harmonica. He played a haunting, blue-note-strewn introduction, then sang in a quiet baritone:

The lad from the northern isles
With salt on his lips
And spray on his cheek
And sea in his eyes
Embraced his inevitable destiny
As father before to fish with his father
Loved the salt and the spray and the sea

The lad from the northern isles
With passion on lips
And blush on his cheek
And love in his eyes
Pursued the girl of his childhood
As husband intent to settle with wife
As generations before to stay in the isles

The girl from the northern isles
With curse on her lips
And rage in her cheek
Forsook her home in the isles
Adventure to seek rejecting her home
And the salt and the spray and the sea

I was watching Jenny, who sat in the corner of the room where she had lit the last lamp. As Lamarre returned to his harmonica for a concluding reprieve of the initial melody, she started to cry.

Colleen had gazed intently at Lamarre while he sang and played. Now as he finished the song and brought the harmonica slowly down from his mouth I heard her murmur, "Sing and play for me, musician man. For me."

But he was tucking his harmonica back into his pocket and seemed not to notice.

The diners began to drift away. The Count and Randy said goodnight and went upstairs to their overnight rooms, saying they'd see me in the morning before we all left.

Sonny and I went out on the veranda to enjoy the night air. He pointed out the lights of Saint John reflecting on the clouds in the distance.

"There's your home," he said.

I gazed at the murky play of lights in the sky, signals from another world. Most of the houses in the city now had electricity. Many had telephones and more and more had radio sets. Motorized transport was forcing the messy horse drawn wagons from the streets. I was accustomed to the welcoming of modernity, to the order and stability of this city world, the source of my security and prosperity. It was a world of dependable work, in the factories and docks and offices, and of predictable relationships.

Turning back toward the lamp lit dining room I saw no evidence that I was in the twentieth century. From my business associates in the city I knew that work in the woods gave only a precarious existence, which might offer prosperity now but only a few years before had been disrupted by mill closures and long layoffs, a cycle which was forecast to resume at any time. The boarding house seemed no more secure, its economic survival apparently dependent upon a few diners from the woods communities and on travellers selling the latest in bathroom ware and ladies' underclothes.

Nodding toward the city lights I said, "It's like another world, isn't it?"

Sonny shrugged. "I wouldn't know. I only know here. It's enough for me, and for most of us out here." He shook my hand and said, "Hope to see you again."

Lamarre appeared on the veranda and also shook my hand, asserting, "We'll meet again, I'm sure."

They left with a group of men returning to the small woods communities scattered along the road between the towns. Some of the diners set off for the late shift at the mill. Megan and Colleen came out.

"'Night, honey," Megan said to me, descending the veranda steps.

Colleen said, "Where's Lamarre?"

"Just left," I said.

"Wouldn't you know it."

The girls set off toward the cabins. The last two diners came out and bade me goodnight. They set off across the meadow, apparently following the girls, who looked back over their shoulders at them, giggling.

I lingered on the veranda, as I'd lingered earlier in the evening. Then I'd been inclined to avoid further involvement with the boarding house. Now I found myself strangely attracted to the world I'd glimpsed that evening. Despite its disturbing aspects—the threat of fire, the directness and sensuality of the girls, especially Jenny, the raving man of God and the diners' undisguised animosity towards him, the stories of marauding bears—despite all this, it seemed a world of kindness and friendship easily offered. My city world seemed dour and cold beside it.

Jenny came to the door, her eyes still red. "Nurse told me you didn't want bed and breakfast. Are you sure?"

"Quite sure, thank you. I have to be on my way very early."

That quizzical look again, head tilted, frowning. Then, abruptly, "Suit yourself. I'll show you to your room now."

Chapter Two

June 1ˢᵗ 1916

I am alone in the woods, with no-one to talk to except you, my journal. I sit on the veranda of the old house, looking across the meadow to the sea, waiting for boarders (who never come). I wonder if I should offer my nursing skills to the few people who live out here in the woods communities. Perhaps that would earn me some income, to supplement what my dear Noel brings when he visits.

Intrigued by the Seashore Boarding House, and restless with the thought of Jenny, I was unable to sleep. In the early hours of the morning, tormented by my wakefulness, I rose from the hard, narrow bed and paced on the bare floorboards. The room held no amusement, being bare except for a night table on which stood a bowl, a jug of water, and an old Harper's Magazine. I peered out of the window but I was at the rear of the boarding house, where the forest pressed close, and I could see only darkness and the vague forms of branches. I decided to try and induce tiredness with a walk outside. I crept downstairs, across the deserted dining room, and let myself out onto the veranda. A full moon shone through fractured clouds, palely lighting the clearing in front of the house. I set off on the footpath across the meadow, playing with a fancy of knocking on Jenny's cabin door and being welcomed in. As I reached the point where the footpath split, the door of her cabin opened. A man emerged. Keeping hidden, I ran down to the shore and threw myself onto the shingle of the beach. I felt the familiar devastation of my affections, even as I cursed my irrationality. I had no affinity with Jenny beyond what I mistook for some flirting on her part and an undoubted but shallow attraction on mine. Certainly I had no claim on her and no reason to be aggrieved at her for consorting with someone else.

But I was aggrieved, and in morose self-pity I nursed the familiar pain. I don't know how long I sat there, perhaps I dozed, before I heard footsteps further along the beach. The moonlight made Nurse's face a ghostly grey and accentuated the lines of tiredness. She sat beside me.

"Mr. Strathearn, I know you have to be up early, but—two a.m.?"

"I couldn't sleep, and thought I'd take a stroll outside, and ..."

"And you saw someone leave Jenny's cabin and you ran down here to sulk. I couldn't sleep either and I watched you."

"I know it's silly and I have no right to feel this way. I thought, simply, Jenny showed some interest in me, and I tried to let her know I was interested too."

"Interested? Mr. Strathearn, you are not in the city now, going through some formal social routine of introductions and flirtations and all those puerile maneuvers that men and women are supposed to go through before they are allowed to become friends. Jenny offered you bed and breakfast, and you refused."

"What has refusing bed and breakfast got to do with the play of relationships?"

"Bed and breakfast is our playful code—playful, but also giving us some protection from prosecution—for requesting the services of the girls—in bed. We are not just a boarding house and clinic here. We are also a brothel. And Jenny is not just a nurse and a chambermaid and a waitress. She is also a prostitute."

I looked at Nurse, shaking my head.

Nurse nodded and said quietly, "Yes. Jenny is a prostitute."

I walked to the water's edge, where I grabbed a handful of shingle and flung it into the waves. Childish, I knew, but I had to express my humiliation in some way. Nurse followed me and we watched the surge and breaking of the waves in silence.

At length she said, "Why are you so angry?"

"I'm not angry. I'm embarrassed. I'm ashamed of my conceit, thinking Jenny was attracted to me. I should have known better. No wonder she was so free with her show of affection."

"Don't be too hard on yourself, or on Jenny."

"Why shouldn't I resent the predations of a prostitute?"

"How many prostitutes do you know?"

"None, until tonight. But I know about them."

"What do you know about them?"

"I know they sell their affections."

"No. They sell their bodies. Their affections have nothing to do with their business."

A distant glimmer of hope, moonlight glinting on a tin roof, pierced the familiar gloom I'd plunged myself into.

"So what was Jenny offering me, her affections or her body?"

"You'll have to decide that for yourself, but …" Nurse's tone softened. "But I might guess, knowing Jenny, that she was offering both her friendship and herself, hoping that having sex with you might include, or lead to, friendship."

I reeled again at the prospect of love with Jenny, even as my common sense still told me to forsake the boarding house and its inhabitants, and to keep my emotions level and intact.

"What makes you say that Jenny was offering me friendship, as well as sex? Do you know her that well?"

"Yes."

"And do you know love that well, living a hermetic existence here, with no husband, no partner?"

Nurse sighed. She sat on the beach and with her finger traced a meandering trail through the shingle. She sighed again, looking up at me. "Oh— I know love."

I cursed my fatuousness. How could she not have known love at some time, probably many times, in her life, with a face and body still so arrestingly beautiful, even in maturity? I sat beside her.

"I'm sorry. I'm being rude. I'm not accustomed to my feelings being in such disarray."

Nurse laughed gently. "We do seem to provoke strong feelings here at the boarding house, what with the girls and their men, and Pastor Oagles and his anger at us. When I came here, I never intended it to be anything more than just a boarding house, you know."

One April evening in the early days of the Seashore Boarding House, with her spirits and her finances at a low ebb, Nurse looked through her accounting book and wondered again whether to give up the boarding house as a hopeless business. She lit the lamps and sat in her office behind the counter. There were no boarders and no diners, and she had just decided there would be no-one in that night when a car drew up outside. Footsteps mounted the veranda steps. The door opened.

She saw, just for a moment, her doctor lover, the same leaning height and greying hair. But her visitor was leaning forward to peer into the room, and as he saw her and stepped into the light, she realized he was younger, broader and fairer than she had thought, and the greying hair was a trick of the light. And his clothes—cord trousers, heavy boots, checked woolen jacket bearing traces of oil or wood sap—were those not of medicine, but of the woods and mill workers. He smiled, and she noted a soft, blonde moustache. He came forward with the awkward confidence that masked shyness and uncertainty.

"Is this the Seashore Boarding House? I need a room for the night. If it's not too late."

He saw a wraith of a woman in the soft shadowed light of the far side of the room. The lamplight exaggerated her paleness and he thought her hair was silver until she looked up and he realized this was the sheen of the lamplight and saw the rich auburn lustre of her hair. The light that angled in around the stairwell carved lines on her forehead and at the corners of her eyes. She was only a few years older than him, but where he felt a burgeoning zest for life and experience, she seemed already wearied and depressed by them. Yet beautiful.

"This is the Seashore Boarding House, and you are not too late, and I do have a room free. In fact I have all my rooms free. You will likely be my only guest," she said.

He signed the guest book and said he was heading for Saint John to join a ship leaving next week. He had heard of the Seashore Boarding House from friends who travelled that route. Didn't often travel that way himself, though. She never saw him again, after that one night.

"I could eat, if that's all right," he said, with awkward boldness.

She prepared supper for him and leaning over him to lay down his plate encountered his eyes only inches from hers, holding hers with their liveliness.

"You look tired," he told her. "Please sit down. Join me."

She watched him eat, energetically and voraciously, envying him his unfettered exuberance. She wished she could recapture the energy she had felt when she started living in the woods, wished she did not feel so drained by the worry of running the boarding house and by the demands of her patients. She wished she could be possessed by vigour.

She realized he was talking to her.

"… Lonely here, so few customers. D'you ever get bored?"

"I'm too busy to get bored. I don't just run the boarding house. I do some nursing, too."

"You're too busy for your own good, if you ask me. You look worn out."

She half rose and reached for his plate to take it out but he caught her hand boldly, looked at her timidly, said, "I'll take my plate to the kitchen and I'll make some coffee. You call and tell me where things are."

He brought coffee for them both and found her crying, made defenceless and weak by his kindness.

"Tough going, eh?" was all he said, and she found she had stood, and fallen against him as he quickly set the cups down, spilling coffee, freeing his hands to enclose her and to pat her back as if she was a hurt child. The pats became strokes, which became insistent and rhythmic as they moved lower, shaping her tiredness to his energy. He picked her up and carried her upstairs to her room. It was eight months since she had

been with her lover and she accepted the stranger with the passion of her resentment and frustration. He lay breathless, astonished.

In the morning, invigorated, she crept downstairs before he woke and made breakfast for him. He ate silently and hurriedly because he had to be in Saint John by eight to sign on for his ship. As he put on his jacket to leave, Nurse told him, "You are the first boarder I have given breakfast to. Usually my guests are in too much of a hurry to eat in the morning."

He laughed and passed her two ten dollar bills from his wallet.

She protested: "It's only ten dollars for the room."

"The rest's for... you know."

"I can't take it. It'd be like I'm a ..."

"I'll tell you what, then." He took back the money. "This is for my bed." He passed her ten dollars. "And this is for the breakfast." He passed her ten more. He kissed her on the cheek and left.

A few weeks later a boarder asked Nurse for bed and breakfast. She told him the boarding house did not serve breakfast. He demurred. A friend, a seaman, had told him bed and breakfast was available and well worth the extra money. She hesitated and accepted. In the morning he left in a hurry without eating.

Randy Fudge greeted her on his next visit with, "Expanding business, I hear. Congratulations. I wish I could expand mine. Would you be putting me down for the bed and the breakfast tonight, please, m'darling?"

Nurse concluded, "So now you know, Mr. Strathearn. Myself, I've more or less retired from that part of the business. But the girls still use the code. It just sort of stuck."

I wanted to ask more, about those early days, about her lover, about how she came to live in this isolated place. But having told the story, she grew quiet. She lay back on the beach, shaping her body to the pattern of the shingle, and her eyes closed. I leaned back on my elbows, watching her. She fell asleep, her hair spread fan-like around her, one arm touching my shoulder, the other flung across the rocks. Another injured gull. As I looked down at her, she awoke, and said, cryptically and inconsequentially, "Jenny will not love you, I warn you. She will be the warmest friend you will ever have, but she will not love you."

Before I could ask why, she fell asleep again, and I was left feeling even more bewildered about my feelings for Jenny. Eventually I, too, dozed, and when I woke the sun rising behind the boarding house was tinting the furthest islands out in Pocomoonshine Bay. Nurse's clothes lay beside me and she was waving from beyond the rocks where the seals lay. I looked back at her clothes and realized she was naked. I hesitated only a moment before shedding my city modesty and joining her in the same state in the water, gasping at its coldness. It was impossible to stay in long and we supported each other as we walked on the slippery pebbles through the shallows. At that moment the door of Jenny's cabin opened. She stretched, waved, and went back inside. Nurse thanked me for my company and suggested I ask Jenny for tea. Still naked, she collected her clothes and set off across the meadow toward the boarding house, while I dressed, crossed to Jenny's cabin, and knocked timidly at the door.

When she opened it I blurted out, "We didn't make love."

She laughed. "Nurse and you? I know that."

"And I didn't know that bed and breakfast meant ... what it means here."

"You surprise me."

"I didn't even know the boarding house existed until yesterday afternoon. I'm sorry if my refusal offended you." I hesitated, then added, "I wish I had understood."

"Well, now that you know our code, you know what to say if you return."

"I'll return—tonight, if I may—for bed and breakfast with you."

She smiled. "Of course."

I felt foolishly dizzy again, as I had when she stood close to me the night before.

"Will I be just a client?"

"What else would you be?"

I hung my head, too constrained by formal manners to say that I already longed to be her lover and her friend. Jenny took pity on my awkwardness and said, severely but kindly, "You may imagine yourself more than just a client, and you may pretend that I am foolishly and hopelessly enraptured by you. I may even pretend that, too. But remember, it will be only pretence."

She took my hand, said, warmly now, "Come in and have some tea and breakfast."

She pulled me inside, just as she had pulled me into the dining room the night before. Using my hand for support, she stood on a chair to reach for an extra cup on a high shelf. I released her hand so that I could hold her waist lightly, to steady her. She stepped down, turning to face me as she did so. My arms encircled her waist. We stood for a moment. She said, "Well now," and drew me into her bedroom. And we had Seashore Boarding House bed and breakfast, then and there.

Afterwards she promised to honour our evening arrangement and I drove to Saint John, where I started my day's work with the anticipation of Jenny's melting nakedness hanging like a gauzy curtain between my city and business world and the world of the Seashore Boarding House.

Chapter Three

At noon I strolled from my office near the city centre to Katy's Kitchen on the Korner on Union Street, where I often ate lunch and supper. As I walked, my surroundings changed, from the tall office buildings, bright shops and wide streets of the city centre to the row houses, corner stores and narrow streets of the warehouse and docks area. Katy's Kitchen was far enough away from the city centre and close enough to the docks and warehouses to be patronized by the stevedores and warehousemen who worked there, rather than by the executives and clerks from the banks and offices of the centre. Although I dined alone and rarely spoke to anyone at Katy's Kitchen, I felt at home and relaxed there. Katy herself served me at my usual window table and I was half way through my meal when I was surprised to see Theodore Delap, a business acquaintance, gesturing to me through the window. He refused my waved invitation to come in, so I went outside to him.

"Mr. Delap, what are you doing in this part of town?"

"I'm returning from business at the McLennan Warehouse, my boy. But I should ask you—ah—what are you doing in a place like this—ah—Katy's Kitchen? There are far better meals to be had in the centre, in far more—ah—congenial surroundings."

I shrugged. "I like it here."

He put a hand on my shoulder and looked me steadily in the eye. He was considerably older than me, a well established lawyer and financier, president of both the Bar Association and the City Association of Business and Professional Executives, the two professional organizations to which I belonged and in which membership was essential for business success in the city. He looked upon any aspiring lawyers and businessmen in Saint John as his personal protégés and protectorates.

He went on, "But you seem to be one who is not too—ah—particular about his surroundings. I hear you had an interesting night, my boy."

He continually interrupted his speech with 'my boy' and 'ah', so that it was at once both avuncular and accusatory.

"What do you mean?"

He clasped his hands behind his back and strode to and fro on the sidewalk as if he was delivering a lecture. "You stayed at that rural estab-lishment, the—ah—Seashore Boarding House, last night."

"How did you hear that?"

"Word travels fast, my boy, even through empty woodland. Have you been there before?"

I told him the circumstances of my stay, although he seemed to know them already. He stopped pacing and put his hand on my shoulder again.

"Let me advise you, my boy, on behalf of the people we work with, our sort of people, you understand, those in the legal and business world of the city. Let me advise you that the Seashore Boarding House is not a desirable place to visit, let alone to—ah—stay at, even in an emergency. The people associated with it are, shall we say, morally—ah—careless, lacking belief in any received system of virtue. They are poor, ragged crea-tures, a different species, to be pitied, perhaps, but not to be associated with by you and me."

"They seemed pleasant and helpful to me."

"They may—ah—seem so. But it's a form of subtle—ah—seduction. No, my boy, it's not a place for you. We want you and your business to be a success. We want you to be one of us ..."

His arm was around my shoulders now, as we paced to and fro on the sidewalk.

"... And associating with places and people like that, and like this—ah—this Katy's Kitchen place, is not going to help further you or your business. We're thinking of your best interests, my boy."

Katy put her head around the door of the café. "Your lunch is getting cold, dear. Do you want me to keep it warm for you?"

Theodore Delap frowned at her, looked back at me, and shook his head. "Take care where you go, my boy, and with whom you—ah—associate." He set off toward the centre, then turned back. "One other thing, my boy. Your—ah—membership fee for the City Association is due, has been for a month. Pay up, my boy."

He wagged his finger in mock threat.

"What do I get for my money?"

I had intended to respond in a similarly playful tone but something in me, and something in the way he had spoken to me, gave my voice a sardonic edge.

He looked sharply at me. "Membership, my boy. Acceptance. It says you are one of us and your success is—ah—dependent upon your being one of us."

He held my glance until I dropped my eyes and turned away to re-enter the café. As I returned to my table, I saw through the window that he was still looking at me, his fingers thoughtfully stroking his chin.

When I left Katy's Kitchen, I found my way blocked by a horse and dray unloading barrels of molasses, so I turned into Horsefield Lane to avoid the obstruction. The row houses here had split stable-style doors, and two women, with the top half of their door open, leaned over the lower half watching the street. One of them was very young, perhaps fourteen or fifteen, with an acne pocked face and watering eyes. The other was in her forties, at least. They both wore blouses carefully unbuttoned to reveal the top of their brassieres.

The older one surveyed me with heavily shadowed eyes and said, "Looking for something, dear? Something to help you unwind after a busy morning?" She ran a nicotine stained finger across her lips.

I said hurriedly, "No. Certainly not." I walked by quickly, then stopped and looked back. "I apologize. I didn't mean to sound rude. I don't want anything. But thank you for offering."

The older one said, "Any time, dear."

She nudged the young girl, who said, as if reading from a script, "You know where to find us," and looked for approval at the older woman. The older one winked at me. I walked back to them.

"I don't want anything but I'd like to offer you money, anyway."

"No, dear, you can't," the older woman said firmly. "Maud and Mandy won't take it without giving something in return. Are you sure you wouldn't like a little sport, a little business, with both of us together, if you like? Then you can pay us. But something for nothing? No, that's not the way it's done, is it, Mandy?"

Mandy shook her head, looking down.

I thanked them again and said I would remember where to find them.

"You do that," said Maud, and winked again.

Chapter Four

I returned to the Seashore Boarding House and to Jenny that night, and from then on, whenever I travelled between my two offices, which was at least once a week, I stopped at the boarding house.

Sometimes I could plan which day this would be. More often I arrived unannounced, having no way of letting Jenny know I was coming. It was usually late in the afternoon by the time I arrived and the girls would be sunning themselves on the rocks when the weather allowed, sprawling in one of the cabins otherwise. Wherever she was, Jenny seemed to divine my arrival and ran to meet me. My memory conjures the image of her running across the meadow to me, her flimsy white dress floating around her. She would fling herself at me, her arms locking around my neck, her sea scent filling my head.

"Can we have bed and breakfast tonight?"

It was always the first thing I said.

"You don't have to ask."

"Have you anyone booked?"

"Yes, but I'll cancel."

I reeled anew at each encounter.

Sometimes when I arrived, especially if the hour was late, she did not come. Then I knew she was with a client. I'd walk across the meadow and hurry past her cabin, looking carefully out to sea and letting the waves and the wind blot out any sound coming from inside. While I waited, sitting on the beach below her cabin, even in the winter months, I tried to expunge all thoughts of Jenny's occupation from my mind, and all my feelings.

Winter was best for this waiting. As I felt my body freeze I imagined all my feelings freezing with it and I willed my numb fingers and toes, and the chilled lips I could no longer feel, to become a paradigm of my emotions. When Jenny's door at last opened and her client left, I waited until she saw me on the beach. I always refused to look up at the cabin to see her. She had to come to me. It was her atonement, one she did not owe me but which I unreasonably and shamefully demanded from her, and which she granted me in friendship.

No more than friendship.

In summer as I waited my blood raced in the heat with unfair, jealous rage. In vain I fought off images of Jenny's body delivering feigned, practiced passion, torturing myself with thoughts of how much of the same, perhaps, she delivered for me. I envied the seals their cold haven on the rocks and longed for the numbing serenity I imagined the icy water would bring. Sometimes I swam out toward them, but the bone chilling Atlantic brought only leaden, stiffening muscles and no relief from my festering jealousy. I sat at the sea's edge, my eyes on the horizon, and hurled pebbles against the waves.

Her light tread rattling the shingle on the beach betrayed to me what I already knew, that she had seen me and was coming to me at last, knowing that I was ignoring her but forgiving the sulky rage which kept my back to her, my eyes averted, even while I ached to see her, to possess her. Her hands lighted on my shoulders and slid to my neck. She tilted my head back and her lips and hair covered my face as she knelt behind me, pulling me back so that my head rested in her lap.

"My dear, you don't have to wait down here for me. You can wait up at the house, or in one of the other cabins. Why do you torment yourself, sitting here alone?"

"I don't torment myself. You torment me with what you do."

"It's just a job."

"It's supposed to be an expression of love."

"In a romantic and ideal world, maybe. But here at the Seashore Boarding House—it pays some bills."

"I'll pay your bills. I've told you that. I'll pay your share of running the boarding house. Then you won't have to work."

"I have to work in order to be independent and to do my share for the boarding house. I owe that to Nurse and to my friends. And if I don't work—what will that make me? Your own personal prostitute?"

"I would make you my wife if you'd let me."

She released me abruptly, folding her arms and looking away. "How many times do I have to tell you? I will not marry. Marriage is supposed to follow love and I want nothing to do with love."

I sat up, turning towards her. "So you say—but you won't say why."

"I don't have to say why. Why can't you accept that? Why can't you be satisfied with our friendship? What difference would talk of love make to what we have now?" She still looked away from me.

"But I cannot help loving you," I pleaded, knowing I sounded petulant and absurd.

"If you want to be loved, look somewhere other than the Seashore Boarding House." Her severity softened as she turned back to me. "But if you want friendship, if that is enough, then stay, please, because you have that in abundance here."

Megan sat with me once as I waited, and together we watched the sun set behind the islands in the bay.

"Why do you torture yourself like this, honey?" she asked.

I shrugged. "I love Jenny."

"Is it worth it? You could love someone else."

"No. I couldn't."

"Love doesn't exactly fit in with our line of work, you know."

"I'd marry her. She could retire from it. But she refuses to love me."

"Refuses? I don't think love is something you can refuse. You catch it, like you catch the flu. Or it catches you. I don't know how it happens. But I do know it's something you don't—can't—refuse."

"She won't even talk about love."

"Girls like us don't want to talk about love, honey. Love has nothing to do with our business."

But I did talk about love to Jenny. I declared it thoughtfully and rationally, as rationally as one can declare love, as we walked through the meadow or sat on the beach, mindlessly and irrationally as we made love in her cabin or on the beach or in a corner of the meadow when the season and the flies permitted. True to Nurse's warning, and her own, Jenny never declared love for me, though I longed for her to do so, but, true again to Nurse's prediction, she was as warm and true a friend as I could want, and it was easy for me to pretend she felt a shy, secret love for me.

I now spent most weekends at the boarding house, as well as at least one weeknight. Jenny would tell me little of her past but Megan and Colleen were forthright in describing how they came to live and work at the boarding house. Megan was from Eagle Rock, one of the woods communities, and had come to Nurse to be cured, the boarding house code for an abortion, when she was sixteen. When she had recovered, Megan asked how she should pay. Nurse had suggested cooking meals and preparing rooms for guests, and from there, Megan said, "I just sort of expanded my boarding house duties." She added, grinning, "And, honey, I'm good at it."

Colleen reminisced one Sunday afternoon as the girls and I lay on the rocks. We were taking turns describing our earliest memories and she said, "I can remember getting off the boat from Ireland, with my ma and pa, and I remember growing up and going to school back east, around Notre Dame, where we settled."

"What brought you here, then?" Megan asked.

"A musician man," said Colleen.

"We should have guessed," said Megan.

"Tell us about him," Jenny urged.

Colleen breathed in deeply, breathed out and smiled, as if arranging her memories. "He travelled around playing the clarinet. He came to play in the café where I was waitressing. They were a trio, he and his friends, clarinet, bass and piano. Their sign said—the sign they put on the stand when they were playing—*Trio Dolce, Tunes for Dreamers.* You'll never guess what he played every night, especially for me."

Colleen paused, smiling.

Megan and Jenny promptly said together, "When Irish Eyes Are Smiling."

Colleen nodded. "He played it every night, late, and he looked at me all the while he played it."

"Is that all? He played a song for you on the clarinet?" Megan scoffed.

"No. We went out walking and … you know." Colleen paused again.

Megan said, "Go on, then. What happened to Mr. Clarinet?"

"I arrived for work one evening and the sign outside said *Playing Tonight—Duo Dolce.* I thought: What's this? A new band? But it was the same one—except now it was just piano and bass."

Megan and Jenny glanced at one another while Colleen gazed out to sea.

"So good riddance to Mr. Clarinet, eh?" said Megan.

"The bass player said he was playing in the next town."

"Don't tell me you followed him."

"I did."

Megan rolled her eyes. "And I suppose the two of you went out walking again."

"We did."

"And don't tell me. He played When Irish Eyes Are Smiling late at night, just for you."

"He did—until …"

"… Until he moved on again," Jenny supplied as Colleen's voice tailed away.

Colleen nodded.

"How long did this go on?" Jenny asked.

"Two years."

"And then?" Megan prompted.

"He came to Saint John. He was playing at the Harbour Lounge Tea and Beverage Room. I got a job there and on the first night I waited and waited for him to play our tune. But he never did, so I thought, he has no love left for me, not a bit. And when he moved on again—I think he went up to Woodstock—this time I didn't follow."

"Good for you, girl," Megan put in.

All the time she spoke, Colleen gazed out to sea. As she at last turned back to us, I thought I saw the glint of incipient tears in her eyes.

I said quickly, "What brought you here?"

"I kept waitressing in Saint John, but the money wasn't enough to live on. Then I met up with some of the girls from around Horsefield Lane. They used to come in to get away from the cold when the café was quiet and the owner was away. I fell in with them for a while, until I heard about the Seashore Boarding House. I hitched a ride out, and Nurse took me in—me and my experience and skills, that is—and … here I am."

"Here you are," Jenny echoed.

"Here we all are," said Megan, reaching to hug Colleen and Jenny.

At the same time as I became a friend and confidant of the girls, I also became a sort of legal advisor to the boarding house, helping Nurse with a few issues that arose concerning taxes, property, and so on. Then the mill workers began to consult me when they had legal problems and questions.

Nurse watched one night as I sat at my table after supper and a succession of men took turns visiting me to discuss their worries, mostly domestic affairs in which I acted more as social worker than lawyer. I never charged for this. I felt it was repayment for the hospitality I received at the boarding house, and from Jenny, who from the start had never allowed me to pay for my bed and breakfast visits.

When I finished with the last enquiry, Nurse said, "You seem to have become our resident lawyer."

"I'm happy to be that," I replied.

I felt proud of the official status this seemed to bestow. It was as if I was part of the staff, the family, of the Seashore Boarding House.

Chapter Five

Late one summer night in 1930, nearly three years after I'd first visited the Seashore Boarding House, I sat alone in the dining room. I'd arrived after supper and found the boarding house deserted, with a note pinned to the door: *Nurse—visiting patients in Wesserunsett. Colleen and Jenny—delivering a baby in Eagle Rock. Megan—working in her cabin. Boarders—make yourselves at home. All rooms are available.*

A horse drawn cart pulled up in front of the house. I heard, "Thank you, Nurse," and, from Nurse, "Come and fetch me if the baby gets worse."

I made tea and we sat on the veranda watching the moon glinting on Pocomoonshine Bay. Nurse drew her chair close to mine and said, "While we are alone I need to ask something of you, something which has to be a secret."

"I'd do anything I can to help you and the girls and the boarding house. You know that."

"This is to help me. I need you to draw up my will and I want you to be the executor."

I looked at her in alarm and she went on, "Don't worry. Nothing's the matter with me. But dealing so often with children—tonight it was the Hanley youngster, with pneumonia, poor little thing—makes me think of what will happen to the boarding house if I die."

I looked at her again, this time in puzzlement. "What has the future of the boarding house have to do with children? Unless … Are you thinking of bequeathing the boarding house to a child?"

Nurse looked at me steadily.

"Yes. To my own child. I have a child. That is the secret and it must remain so. In the will you will say that the boarding house will be left to the child—all will be revealed then, of course—and as my executor you will find him so that I can make amends for deserting him."

In my surprise I could find nothing to say until, seeing tears starting from Nurse's eyes, I put my arm around her and murmured, "This is a Nurse story I haven't heard."

Wiping her eyes and nestling into my shoulder, Nurse said, "You've heard all about my so called affair, haven't you?"

I nodded. I'd already discovered much of the history of Nurse and the Seashore Boarding House from the girls.

Nurse went on, "What no-one knew when I gave up nursing and left the hospital was that I was pregnant. I went into hiding before I left Saint John to come out here to the boarding house. Noel arranged it. I stayed with his sister in the north end and she helped me with the confinement. Then Noel delivered the child himself.

"He got such a shock when the baby was born. The little boy had a condition known as penis rufus, poor little thing. Noel went straight to his Zwicker's Medical Dictionary. I remember what he read, word for word:

Penis rufus. A very rare form of strawberry mark in which the discoloration pervades, but is confined to, the penis. No dysfunction of the organ is caused, except for occasional discomfort in the form of irritation of the skin during copulation. Medical practitioners will be fortunate indeed if they encounter just one instance of this singular and aberrant eccentricity of nature in a lifetime's work."

"I've never heard of penis rufus," I said. "Poor little thing. What happened to him?"

"Noel took him away as soon as he was born. He'd arranged for him to be adopted. I didn't want to know who was taking him in or where they lived. We agreed our child would always be a secret. When Noel signed the boarding house over to me, I told him—I promised him—I'd always keep the secret, although he said he didn't want me to promise."

"And you've never had contact with the child since the birth?"

Nurse shook her head. I hugged her tightly as she cried again. When she recovered, I ventured, "And Dr. Gallant—Noel?"

"He came to see me a few times and brought me money while I was getting the boarding house set up."

Nurse stood and leaned against the veranda rail, looking across the meadow, then suddenly swung around, her eyes gleaming with tears and remembered passion, so that I saw her as the young woman Dr. Gallant had courted.

"How I loved the waiting for him, when I knew he was coming and I hadn't seen him for a week or two."

She woke early in the morning, knowing it was a special day even before she re-membered why. She luxuriated in the undefined pleasure she anticipated. She lay still and listened to the waves breaking on the rocks and the breeze disturbing the grass in the meadow. She allowed her eyes to wander around her bedroom. It was small, with space for just her bed and a chair. Tiny roses adorned the wallpaper, which was brown and peeling in one corner where the rain had leaked through. Her bed was hard and narrow, so narrow that she and her lover scorned it for their passion, although she longed to wake in it with him beside her, knowing that was impossible.

Yes! That was the reason for her excitement. Today—he was coming!

She swung her feet to the wide floorboards and crossed to the window. She never tired of looking out at the meadow—'her' meadow—and at the sea beyond. Three deer skittered into the trees as her movement disturbed them and a porcupine continued his unhurried way along the track toward the woods road.

How would she spend the time until he came? She had to allot herself tasks through the day to keep herself patient as she waited for him. She told herself: Seven o'clock— breakfast, leisurely on the veranda, watching for the deer and moose on the edge of the meadow, listening for the woodpecker, counting the shades of green among the spruce and fir and pine. Eight o'clock—clean the house and get the rooms ready for guests, although the house was clean and she knew, in those early days of the Seashore Boarding House, that it was unlikely there would be boarders. Ten o'clock—make coffee and take it, leisurely again, down to the beach. The rest of the morning—tend the little garden where she was trying to grow a few vegetables, when the deer and the raccoons allowed. After- noon—chop and split wood ready for the winter, walk to the store in Ratters Lake and buy groceries for the guests she hoped for, with the last of the money Noel had left on his previous visit.

She did all that, and walked slowly back on the dusty, deserted woods road to her boarding house. She found she still had two hours to fill before he came. She strolled across the meadow to the beach. She swam out to the rocks where the seals lay, disturbing them, so that they plunged from the rocks and cavorted in the surf. Then she swam back to shore. It was so deserted at the Seashore Boarding House in those early days that she never bothered with a bathing suit. She simply emerged from the water and laid herself on the rocks to dry, while the seals settled back on the further rocks. As the sun warmed her, she flushed with the anticipation of seeing him and touching him.

She heard his car—she guessed it must be him—as she lay there. She raised her head enough to peer across the beach and through the grass of the meadow to make sure, and lay back. She heard him call, once, "Melody," but she didn't respond. She waited until she heard his feet pause as they stepped from the meadow onto the shingle of the beach, knowing that he was looking at her. She felt her body arch involuntarily with the pleasure of his admiration. She opened her eyes and smiled.

"You knew I was here," he accused.

"I wanted you to find me like this."

She rose and ran to him, ignoring the discomfort of the shingle on her bare feet, feeling his gaze still raking her. She flung herself at him, tumbling them both backwards into the meadow.

Later, as they walked on the shore, he said, "I'm sorry I was so late."

"Don't be sorry. I'm just so happy to see you."

"And I'm sorry, too, that I can't manage to come more often."

"I said don't be sorry."

He was always apologizing, for being late, for not coming more often, for—of all things—disturbing her. In the warm weather they walked in the woods and along the shore, he with his leaning walk, she clinging to his arm. When it was winter they talked and read in the boarding house, beside the woodstove in the dining room, loving their solitude, away from the gossip they'd endured in the city. They made love wherever and whenever they chose, in the woods, in the meadow, on the beach, in the boarding house.

Then, one day in the fall, when she expected him, he did not come.

She accomplished all the tasks she had allotted herself to get through the day until he arrived and still he did not come. She waited on the veranda, pacing, for an hour, growing more and more restless. She went down to the shore, out of sight of the house, telling herself that when she walked back, he would have arrived in her absence. She watched the seals and the gulls, and poked in tidepools, for as long as she could, telling herself: Now he will have arrived at last. He will have called my name in the empty house. He will have guessed I'm on the shore, and will be crossing the meadow to find me, even now.

But when she climbed up from the shore, of course the meadow was empty, and all that day she waited, and he did not come.

He arrived one day the next week, unexpectedly, saying it was becoming harder for him to get away. Usually he told his wife he was working, and she didn't suspect, but now she was sick, and as her illness grew worse, she clung more to him, and he felt bound to stay with her. Melody assured him she didn't blame him for feeling that way.

His visits became fortnightly, monthly, every six weeks, whenever he could get away. And the rarer their times together grew, the more intense they became.

One day she came back from Wesserunsett, from seeing one of her first patients, and found a note from him, tucked under the teapot beside the stove, where he knew she would find it. She read: 'Sorry you were not here. Noel.'

Two months later he arrived unexpectedly at supper time. He entered uncertainly, having seen vehicles outside. It was when boarders were starting to discover the Seashore Boarding House and she was growing busy at last. Randy Fudge and the Count were there for supper and board. The Count took her lover's hesitation for the uncertainty of a newcomer to the boarding house and greeted him.

"My dear sir, do come in. Let me welcome you to the Seashore Boarding House. Please join my colleague, Mr. Randy Fudge, and I at our table."

"A pleasure, m'darling," said Randy, rising and engulfing Dr. Gallant's hand in his. "And you would be?"

"Noel Gallant. Dr. Noel Gallant. I was visiting a patient in—er—Eagle Rock, and as it was getting late I thought I might eat here before driving home."

When Nurse came in—she was Nurse by then, no longer Melody—the Count introduced Dr. Gallant to her. As they shook hands he repeated the lie that he was visiting a patient. Their handshake was brief and he released her hand abruptly. She served them supper and joined them at the table afterwards. Her lover ate quickly, responding only briefly to conversation directed his way by Randy and the Count.

When he rose to leave, she went outside with him. She stood on the top step of the veranda while he held the door of his car.

He said, "I'm sorry you weren't here when I came last time. I waited as long as I could."

She seethed. As if it was her fault, for not being there. But all she said was, "I am sorry, too, but I had work to do. I had to see my patients. You should understand that."

"Of course I understand. I'm sorry. Perhaps next time I come we can find some time to be alone."

"I hope so, but I need my boarders to survive."

She made a little move towards him, to embrace him, but she saw his eyes shift to the window. She followed his glance. Randy and the Count were visible, still at their table. She drew back. He made a small, hopeless gesture with his hands, fluttering them outward. She gave a little wave with her fingers. He climbed in his car, and wound down the window, and said, "Sorry."

"That was the last time I saw him. He just stopped coming and I've not seen him for years."

"And the child?"

"Noel always said the child was doing well. But that was all he'd tell me, and all I wanted to know. I don't know where the boy is or what he's doing. He'd be a teenager now. It's my greatest shame, letting the child go like that, although I know I'd never have been able to care for him."

"Did you think of abortion?" I ventured.

"Oh yes. But there was no-one I trusted in the city and Noel would not risk doing it himself. There were places where girls could go but they were not safe. That's one reason I started doing abortions here, because if I had decided to do it—to have an abortion—there should have been somewhere for me to go. And there is a need for it, out here. As soon as people knew I did nursing, they would come and ask."

"Didn't you need special instruments and equipment?"

"I brought the little equipment I owned with me when I left the city, and you can always improvise, you know. It was disposal that was the problem."

"Disposal of the ... babies?"

"The fetuses, yes. I buried them in the woods. The next day, all I used to find was a hole with paw marks all around. The bear ..."

"The Bear Pots bear?"

"The same, I guess. Well, I suppose the bear helped me with disposal. I can't say I liked it, but I didn't know what else to do. I kept on burying them, and he kept on helping himself. What else could I do?"

"And you called doing abortions, curing, as a sort of precaution."

"Another code—yes. We seem to live by codes—curing, bed and breakfast—as if we are ashamed of what we do."

"You live by a code of helping, and camaraderie, and friendship. That's what I see at the boarding house, and I don't see it when I'm in the city."

Megan and Sonny walked up from the cabins at the same time as a horse and buggy appeared on the track from the highway, Colleen and Jenny whooping with the driver, whom I recognized as an occasional diner from Eagle Rock. He leaped from the buggy and handed the girls down with a huge and gracious bow. They curtsied in return, giggling. He thanked them, swung the buggy around and drove into the night.

"It was a girl," Colleen announced, adding, unnecessarily, "And we've been celebrating."

Jenny sat on my lap and said, "What have you and Nurse been up to?"

I looked at Nurse and raised my eyebrows.

"Just talking over old times," she said, her eyes still shining.

Chapter Six

One morning I stayed late at the boarding house. The overnight guests had left and the girls were busy upstairs when there was a knock at the door.

It was nearly six years since my encounter in the woods with Pastor Calvin Oagles but I recognized him at once. He must have walked in from the highway to the boarding house, the exercise having no more effect on his clothing than the first time I saw him. He was dressed the same, black suit, with a red handkerchief in the breast pocket, except that now a red tie augmented the colour. We often heard of his preaching in the city, where he virulently denounced those he deemed sinners, and of his growing band of followers, but we had experienced no direct contact with him. We did, however, receive occasional reports of his being seen on the highway near the boarding house, ranting at it in the same manner as when I first saw him. He'd even ventured to visit and preach in some of the woods communities, where he had received unsympathetic hearings. Now he stood on the veranda steps, smiling at his reflection in the window, patting his hair into careful unruliness. He turned his smile on me as I opened the door.

"So this is the famous Seashore Boarding House." He surveyed the front of the house from side to side and from roof to veranda as he spoke, as if assessing its worth.

"This is the Seashore Boarding House, yes, but—famous?"

"Oh yes—famous. At least in some quarters." He looked me up and down. "And you have found your way here. I knew you would."

"Why do you say that?"

He advanced on me, raising one finger as if his speech was a reprimand. "Because when we met before, you were wandering in a desert of unbelief. You had no convictions to sustain you against the convictionless and you had to be drawn here, despite my warning."

"Your warning?"

He stood before me in the doorway, so close that instinct told me to step aside but I held my ground, barring his entrance into the house. He still held one finger raised.

"I proclaimed to you: Either learn—or prepare to burn. You failed to learn." He looked around. "You are quite among the trees here. Don't you fear a forest fire?"

"There is little anyone can do about a forest fire."

I was aware of Nurse standing behind me and now Pastor Oagles directed his speech at her, ignoring me.

"But you can. I, saith the Lord, will be unto her a wall of fire round about. You can be purified and saved and live here secure in the knowledge that if fire should come, while it may be a consuming, jealous fire for some, it will be a security for you."

Misplaced manners made me move aside so that I no longer stood between Nurse and Oagles. As soon as I moved he entered the boarding house, brushing past Nurse, proclaiming as he went, "Yes, even when thou walkest through the fire, thou shalt not be burned. But to achieve this grace, you must repent and be purified and believe."

"I believe, in a manner of my own choosing, and ..." Nurse started.

Pastor Oagles interrupted. "Some strange, erratic belief, no doubt, unformed, frayed and ragged, strange fire to offer before the Lord." He strutted around the room as he spoke as if, again, assessing the value of the property.

Nurse continued, "And as for repenting, I have nothing to repent."

Oagles had stopped beside the counter, looking up the stairs. Now he whirled around to face Nurse. "You have no visitors here?"

"Of course I have visitors. This gentleman is one of them. This is a boarding house."

"And you must know, then, that your visitors offend my Lord."

"I cannot help that."

A subtle, invisible shift of eyes and teeth turned his smile into a sneer of anger and contempt. His finger admonished again.

"I came here to offer you the chance of grace. I wanted to present you with the gift of repentance and purification that I have been bringing to the people of the communities around here."

"I do not need repentance and purification."

His voice rose as he marched toward Nurse, his finger pointing and gesticulating. "People visit here for sinful purposes, to indulge their animal carnality and to be divested of the fruit therefrom."

I intervened, "Your speech amounts to assault. I suggest you stop immediately."

He ignored me, raising his voice further. "I warn you, both of you, that you *will* repent and change your ways or your sins will be judged in the fire of my Lord. For the Lord thy God is a consuming fire, even a jealous God, who maketh his angels spirits and his ministers ..." He stood still and indicated himself. "... A flame of fire."

I had moved between Nurse and Oagles, so that now he was raving at her over my shoulder. I was wondering whether I should cast aside my city inhibitions and threaten him when the sound of a vehicle approaching arrested his speech. Randy's familiar van, with *Worley Washes the World* emblazoned on the side, appeared.

"Leave—now, sir," I said.

Pastor Oagles glanced at me and at the van, then resumed quietly, speaking directly at Nurse. "Dear lady, fear for your sins. For the Lord rained upon Sodom and Gomorrha brimstone and fire. Lord's ire feeds the fire. This you will learn—or prepare to burn."

Randy's bulk loomed in the doorway. Nurse stepped back so that she was close beside him. Pastor Oagles stepped around me and offered his hand to Randy.

"Would you be leaving now, or would you be wanting some assistance to your car?" Randy asked him, ignoring his hand.

Pastor Oagles turned back to me and smiled. Then he smiled, too, at Nurse and Randy.

"You'll be leaving, then?" Randy prompted. He folded his arms, glared at Oagles, and stepped aside, his eyes not leaving the minister. Oagles walked slowly past. He stopped on the veranda, looked back and nodded and smiled at Nurse, and set off toward the highway. We watched him until he was out of sight. Nurse leaned against Randy and he put his arm around her.

"I came back to visit the outhouse, m'darlings, antiquated facility though it may be. I didn't expect to meet our friend Oagles," he said lightly.

I was shaking, I wasn't sure whether with anger or fear.

With the help of a private investigator who often worked for my practice, I researched Pastor Calvin Oagles. Carmen Burns's report landed on my desk six months—and five hundred dollars plus expenses—later:

First known address of Calvin Oagles: "The Scarlet Stocking" (a bordello, no longer in existence, although the building still stands and now houses a vegetarian restaurant), Silver City, British Columbia.

Mother: Miss Gillian Maud Robbins, a.k.a. Groaning Gilly. Deceased.

Father: Unknown.

Miss Robbins's former colleague at The Scarlet Stocking, Miss Susan Andrews, formerly known as Whiplash Sue, now 92 and resident at "Sunny Haven", Prince Rupert, British Columbia, in interview: "I remember young Calvin, yes. Always in trouble, he was. In trouble for peeking through keyholes at us girls when we were working. He peeked at his ma, too. Groaning Gilly, that'd be. We played a joke on him, to teach him a lesson not to be peeking at us. Next time we caught him peeking at his ma and her man—a client, you know—we crept up behind him and held a candle to his bum. Didn't mean to harm him, of course, just give him a surprise and a fright. But his pants caught fire and he got burned and we were all in trouble with the madam. It cured him, though—'cept that he started a new habit. Instead of peeking through keyholes, he started peeking through this heating vent into his ma's room upstairs. He had to stand on the stove to do it. 'Course he couldn't stay there long, because the stove was always lit, it being cold up there in Silver City. So he peeked for as long as he could stand it. Then his ma caught him at it, and got so mad she made him stand on the stove for ten minutes, to cure him of it for ever, she said. We told her it was wrong, it was too harsh, but she kept us out of the room, until we couldn't stand it any longer. We rushed in, us girls, but the boy was just standing there, on the hot stove, not moving. He says to us, "The fire's burned through my feet. My insides are on fire", but calmly, like, as if he wasn't hurting. His ma was suddenly sorry and grabbed him down and hugged him. Still he wasn't crying or nothing. She looked in his eyes, thinking she'd see tears. And she saw—we all saw, though it's hard to believe and you'll think I'm a crazy old woman telling you this—we saw fire in his eyes. Then he started to speak. I even remember what he said, word for word, because it was from the Bible, from Revelations, and I know my Bible, sir, always have, although the boy didn't, he'd never read it, but he said, like he was a preacher, "His eyes were as a flame of fire and his feet like unto fine brass, as if they burned in a furnace, and his voice was the sound of many waters." Then he looks at his ma and says—it makes me shudder to remember and I still see his eyes, roaring with fire—"One day, for your sins, you too will burn." Then out of the house he marches, on his burned feet, and we never saw him again."

Young Calvin was taken into care by local authorities.

He claims later to have attended Western Baptist College, but no records substantiate this.

He held a stewardship at Mission, a farming community in Alberta. Reformed and renamed the ministry the Mission of the Ardent Calefactory. Left in some controversy regarding extremity of his preachings and beliefs.

Founded Ministry of the Pyrotechnical and Fanatical Dogmatists in St. Benedict, Saskatchewan, but resigned following similar controversy.

Next traced to Field, Manitoba, where the church whose ministry he assumed burned down shortly after his arrival. Some controversy over insurance claim, but when this was settled a new church was built, called The Church of the Incendiary Zealots.

Arrived in Saint John in 1929. Joined up with a breakaway church group who found their own church too liberal, ecumenically and socially. Assumed leadership and named the group the Disciples of Fire. Took over the old Dominion Theatre last year, 1933, and named it the Tabernacle of the Disciples of Fire.

Congregation (regular attendees at the Tabernacle) estimated to be well over one thousand. Larger congregation (i.e. those listening regularly to weekly radio sermon, occasional attendees, all those who consider themselves "Disciples of Fire") estimated to be over 6,000. Includes many influential people of the city, councillors, police, teachers, etc.

Respectfully submitted: Carmen Burns, Investigative Services Inc.

Chapter Seven

That summer—it was 1934—was hot, dry and windy. Driving out of St. Stephen and into the woods one afternoon I felt uneasiness rising in me until I could smell my own sweat although I shook as if with cold. I stopped by the road trying to determine why I felt such overwhelming anxiety. What did I fear? I felt as I did when faced with a difficult court case before a hostile judge, adrenaline pulsing in me even while nausea threatened. But I had no difficult work facing me that day. In fact I had only pleasure to anticipate. I was heading to Saint John with the intention of spending the night with Jenny on the way. Was I anxious, I wondered, that I might find her with a client? But no—I remembered—she knew I was coming. She would save herself for me. What, then, was I sensing that was disturbing me so severely?

I drove slowly on.

Stopped again.

Got out of the car. Sniffed the air.

Yes. There it was, the source of my foreboding. Faint and elusive, but unmistakable. The smell of smoke. The harbinger of forest fire.

The wind?

Damn it. From the east. The direction in which I was driving. It would take the fire toward the Seashore Boarding House.

To the woods dwellers—I now counted myself among them, as a regular visitor to the boarding house—forest fire produced a visceral fear, which we accepted and lived with, just as the woods workers lived with the daily threat of injury and maiming. Confronted with fire, we turned feral. Felt a premonition of it. Sniffed it. Assessed the kindling danger. Nodded knowingly. Dispassionately went about the business of survival. Water in buckets around the house. Ladder to the roof at the ready. Buckets on the roof. Shovels to hand. Animals freed. Horses hitched. Trucks and wagons loaded for flight.

The fear of fire was compounded now, for the boarding house and for the woods dwellers who frequented it, by the whiff of Oagles's threats.

I drove on, fast. The smell became stronger. Travelling a ridge of high land I saw smoke in the distance, roiling upwards in black and grey waves. It disappeared from my sight as the road descended but soon the sky was obscured by it and as I neared the boarding house ashes filled the air like swarms of flies.

I skidded as I avoided a porcupine—was he doomed, anyway? —and turned off the woods highway on to the boarding house track. Six deer fled across the meadow as I stopped at the veranda. Megan ran down the steps and pulled the car door open before I switched off the ignition.

"Charlie told me to send anyone who came to help with the fire," she shouted. "It's a half mile east. Randy and the Count have just left for it. You may catch up to them."

I drove back to the road and turned toward Saint John. I soon found Charlie directing the fire fighting from his command post on the highway. Sonny and Lamarre threw me equipment and I ran to join Randy and the Count, who were already at work. For nearly an hour we fought the flames and, helped by a lull in the wind, were gaining control when I heard the shouts.

"Lord's ire ignites the fire."

Through the spiralling smoke and the dying flames Pastor Oagles strode, still dressed predominantly in black, except that now he wore red socks and shoes to match the red tie and pocket handkerchief. Behind him marched a dozen men and women, dressed completely in black. They chanted a liturgy with their leader.

"Lord's ire ..." Pastor Oagles called.

"Ignites the fire," the response came.

"You will learn ..."

"Or prepare to burn."

Charlie shouted, "You set fire, started conflagration."

He strode to the front of his fire fighters to confront Oagles. The men abandoned their work and began to move from their scattered positions to a phalanx behind Charlie. They gripped their shovels tighter as the pastor and his followers approached. Somewhere behind us we heard fire-weakened limbs crash into the forest. The wind whipped ashes and smoke over us and into our eyes.

"Who do you think you are, to threaten the boarding house like this?" the Count demanded, shouting against the wind.

"No, my friend, we threaten nobody," Pastor Oagles asserted. "This fire is but God's cleansing work. There is no danger to those that do not grieve our Lord. For I will bring them through the fire, saith the Lord, and will refine them as silver is refined, and will try them as gold is tried. I will say …" —Oagles stopped and extended his arms as the disciples lined up on each side of him—" … it is my people."

Charlie stopped, too, ten feet from the line of disciples. We stopped behind him. A sudden downdraft swirled smoke between the disciples and us, then whipped it away, leaving my eyes stinging and watering.

"You're perverts, damn you," Sonny snarled.

One of the disciples sneered back, "You're the ones who are damned. You and the diseased whore at that boarding house."

Randy strode forward. With one hand he grasped the lapels of the disciple's jacket. He plucked the man from the line as if landing a fish and held him inches from his face.

"Would you be minding your manners, m'darling man, or would you like a clipped ear?" he growled.

Randy set his victim back on the ground. The disciple straightened his clothing, easing his shoulders into his jacket. He looked at Oagles, who nodded. The disciple said, "We welcome the threats of the ignorant as we undertake the work of our Lord. She is a diseased whore. She is damned. She needs our help."

Randy grabbed the man again. He lifted him and threw him toward Pastor Oagles. The man crashed to the ground, striking his head on a smouldering stump. Behind Randy's back, one of the disciples grabbed a branch from the ground and ran at him. Lamarre threw himself at the assailant. He seized the branch with one hand before it could fall on Randy's head and held the man around the neck with the other. As they fell, the disciple swung his free hand once and caught Lamarre on the cheek, snapping his head back onto the ground as they landed. He raised his fist to strike again but Sonny seized him and held him fast. Lamarre lay still.

Disciples and woodsmen glared at each other.

Fire leapt from the scrub behind the disciples to a pine tree standing solitary and unscathed among the blackened spruce around it. The flames raked from the lowest boughs to the crown in a roaring mass. Sparks and ash showered around us.

Charlie growled, "Get away before lose temper, take off before get angry. No reason your presence, no cause you be here."

"We have work to do here," said Pastor Oagles.

"No-one round here wants follow your beliefs, obey your convictions."

"That is why we have work to do here. They commit adultery and assemble themselves by troops in the harlot's house. There are sinners here and they must be brought to belief."

"Oh—we believe. Own beliefs," Charlie protested.

"Beliefs in what?" Pastor Oagles taunted. Receiving no response, he went on, "So you are a group of believers without a belief. Join us in our crusade, my friends, and find your Lord, lest the land fall to whoredom, and the land become full of wickedness. Or will you stay a bunch of godless, ragamuffin believers?"

I looked around at my friends, the loggers and the mill workers in their greasy, torn work clothes, the travellers' suits dirtied by soot and sweat. I looked back at the disciples. They were immaculate, despite the fire, and despite the idiosyncrasy of their black outfits.

"A bunch of godless, ragamuffin believers," Pastor Oagles repeated for the approval and amusement of his followers. "A bunch of ragged believers."

The disciples looked at each other, nodding and laughing.

"The ragged believers. I guess that'd be us," said Sonny quietly, still holding the disciple in a relentless grip.

A tall spruce beside him, stripped of foliage by the fire, swayed in the wind. From the corner of my eye I saw it lean toward us, straighten, lean the other way, straighten. Sway toward us again. No-one moved, woods workers or disciples. The tree straightened. Swayed the other way yet again. Swayed further. Fell in a crash of splintering boughs. Ash, dirt and smoke swirled into our eyes and settled in our hair and on our shoulders.

"The ragged believers of the Seashore Boarding House," Randy murmured. "Yes, m'darlings, that'd be us."

Lamarre groaned and stirred. The wounded disciple, Randy's victim, still lay where he had landed. The fire crew glanced at Lamarre and the disciples at their motionless comrade. The groups edged towards each other. And through the smoke, walking between the groups, came Nurse. She glanced once at Pastor Oagles, then knelt beside the wounded disciple. The pastor strode forward. Charlie started towards him, throwing his shovel aside and clenching his fists.

Nurse said to Charlie, "Stop." Then to Pastor Oagles she said quietly, "Please leave, you and your people, before someone else is injured." After a moment's hesitation, Oagles gestured to two of his disciples to help the wounded man up. Nurse stopped them.

"This man needs immediate treatment. I will look after him. Now go."

Pastor Oagles glared down at her, then turned and strode away. His disciples followed. As they left he turned and called, "Jezebel."

"Harlot," the disciples responded.

"You will burn with your sins."

"Some day you will burn."

"If you profane yourself by playing the whore ..."

"You shall be burnt with fire."

Nurse ignored them and spoke to the wounded disciple, holding his bloody head in her arms. "Do you feel well enough to walk with the help of these men?"

The disciple opened his eyes and snarled, "Jezebel."

"Help him, please. Take him to the boarding house," she ordered Charlie.

"Leave the bastard here," Sonny muttered.

"Help him, please, Charlie, Count, Randy."

Charlie and the Count obeyed, picking up the man and carrying him to the Count's Hudson, while Randy helped Lamarre to his feet.

Nurse rose and looked at Lamarre's wound. "Bring him along, too," she told Randy.

At the boarding house she cleaned and stitched the disciple's wound, a long gash in the forehead, and told him, "If your headache persists, or if your vision gets blurred, go to the hospital in Saint John immediately."

"I'll go to the hospital anyway," he snapped, rising to leave. "I don't trust the hands of a harlot to have any healing power."

I was standing in the doorway, blocking his exit. "Nurse doesn't charge for her help, but expressions of thanks are always welcome," I told him.

"You get nothing from me but my contempt."

He went to push past me.

"Are all your colleagues as pig-headed as you?" I asked, stepping aside.

"My colleagues are as unyielding and proud in their beliefs as I am. You should open your mind to our beliefs instead of clinging so fiercely to your brutish habits."

He was half way across the veranda when he stopped and turned, producing a pamphlet from an inner pocket and offering it to me. He said warmly, as if remembering his missionary duty, "You must come to one of our meetings and learn about us and our beliefs. You will be welcomed, I promise you."

When I refused it, he laid it on a chair and left.

After watching him go, I picked it up, out of curiosity, and read:

Tabernacle of the Disciples of Fire
Share the Fellowship and the Blessings of Our Family
Be Purified by the Fire of the Lord and Be One of Us
Join Pastor Calvin Oagles for Prayers and Inspiration
Wednesdays at 7 p.m.
Corner of Water and Union

I tucked the pamphlet into my pocket and returned to the nursing room. Colleen was cleaning the gash on Lamarre's head, standing close to him. Nurse watched.

"He was big, six three or six four at least ..." Lamarre recounted.

"Oh my," Colleen murmured, washing dirt and ash from the cut.

"... Near as big as Randy. He would have killed him with that branch. Well it was more like a whole limb. I thought, I've got to save Randy."

"Uh-huh," Colleen put in. She looked closely at the wound. Stepped back. Looked at Nurse for approval.

Nurse nodded. "That's good and clean. I'll close it up."

Colleen stood behind Lamarre and held his head while Nurse stitched the wound.

"So I jumped him," Lamarre went on. "Got hold of the limb with one hand. Got him round the neck with the other."

"Heavens," Colleen said.

"That would have been the end of it except I tripped and … And then Nurse was there."

"You will do," said Nurse. "Let me know if you still have a headache in the morning and if you find you have lost any of your memory."

"I hope you'll remember how to play your whistle and sing your songs, musician man," said Colleen, moving in front of Lamarre, her hands still cradling his head.

Jenny took my hand and led me across the meadow to her cabin. She was wearing her red sash.

"Shouldn't you take that off, or do you consider me part of your duties?" I asked.

She removed it, saying severely, "I don't come to you from any sense of duty. You know that perfectly well."

"Why do you come to me, then?" I continued, trying to keep my voice light and bantering.

"Out of friendship, of course. You know that, too. Isn't that enough for you?"

"In one way, yes, it is enough. I've told you that many times. But—it isn't enough. You must see that. I wish you would come to me out of love as well as friendship. And even if you can't manage love, I still wish you would come with me into the city and live with me."

"We've talked about this before. I don't want to go into the city. I'm happy here, and I belong here. My work is here."

"But that doesn't mean you can never leave the place. I'd like your company in the city as well as here. I'd like your company all the time."

"That sounds suspiciously like a proposal."

"Well it is. Please live with me. Marry me."

"No! How can I be married and do my work?"

70

"You wouldn't have to work if you married me. Your work torments me."

She softened, turning to me, taking my arm and drawing me close.

"I know, and I'm sorry. But this is my world, at the boarding house, and I have to do my part for the business. I owe that, out of friendship to Nurse and the others. It's what I believe I have to do. And I can't help not loving you."

"But why?"

She shook her head and went on, "And if I can't love you, then I won't marry you. But I am—I always will be—your very best friend."

I had to be content with that, and with bed and breakfast in her cabin that night.

Chapter Eight

The next evening, bored in my apartment in Saint John, I discovered in my pocket the pamphlet left by the wounded disciple. On impulse, as it was Wednesday and nearing seven o' clock, I decided to find out for myself something about the Disciples of Fire. I walked to the corner of Water and Union and found the tabernacle. The old stone building had two imposing but useless pillars at either side of its double doors. Between them, at the top of a flight of steps, a podium had been set up and beside it stood a sort of crucible. A small crowd had gathered at the foot of the steps.

As I watched from the opposite corner, the doors swung open and Pastor Calvin Oagles strode to the podium, flanked by two of the disciples I recognized from the encounter in the woods. As he grasped the podium, his jacket fell open, revealing that his shirt was red tonight, as well as his tie and handkerchief and shoes and socks. A few passersby stopped but nothing happened until from the road behind me I heard a shout: "Lord's ire ignites the fire. We will be purified."

Pastor Oagles and his followers at the podium took up the chant. "Lord's ire ignites the fire. We will be purified."

A column of fire shot up from the crucible, apparently ignited by Pastor Oagles himself with a casual wave of his hand.

The marching column, which bore out Carmen Burns's report that Pastor Oagles's immediate followers numbered well over a thousand, reached the steps of the tabernacle and spread themselves before the podium. The street was partly blocked, as well as the sidewalks, so that traffic and pedestrians became part of the crowd.

Pastor Oagles started quietly. "There is a brothel in the woods not a hundred miles from here. Your sons and husbands and fathers are welcomed there. They commit adultery and assemble themselves by troops in the harlot's house. I do not condemn them for their visits, for we are all

subject to the temptations of the flesh. Some of you before me now ..."
His accusing finger suddenly stabbed at figures in the crowd and he
shouted, "Some of you have been there." His voice was quiet again as he
continued. "I do not condemn you. Temptation is part of the Lord's plan
for us. It is His way of testing us, to determine our worthiness to take our
place in His garden. We can pass this test in three ways. We can submit to
temptation, then repent and punish our temptress. Or we can resist. For
this is the will of God, even your sanctification, that ye shall abstain from
fornication. Or we can, all of us, root out temptation and destroy it.

"So let us purify those who would tempt us!

"Let us examine the ways of destroying the temptations of Satan!"

His voice dropped almost to a whisper, and the crowd leaned forward
to hear.

"I have been tempted, like you. I have fallen, like you. I abase myself
before my God and before you and declare myself a miserable sinner, a
tool of the fleshly desire Satan has inflicted on us, and which my Lord
allows to tempt us yet to strengthen us. I am mortal. I am weak. I have
indulged my carnality. I am ashamed. You see before you an abject sinner,
whose only hope of salvation and forgiveness is to grovel in shame before
his God and before you, weeping tears of humility and abasement."

He stopped. He was sobbing, apparently overcome with emotion. The
crowd was silent, absorbed, breathlessly awaiting each murmured word.

Pastor Oagles, between sobs, continued, "Whose only ... hope of salvation ... is ... is ..."

I had to lean forward to hear the almost inaudible voice. I was riveted,
like the crowd, and despite myself, by the intensity of Pastor Oagles's emotion, real or feigned. Suddenly the flame, which had died down, leaped up
again and he plunged both hands into the fire and cried, "... Is to purify
the flesh of the Lord." He withdrew his hands and held them high for the
crowd to see.

The disciples, on cue, took up the chant: "Purify the flesh of the Lord."

"Is not my word like as a fire, saith the Lord."

"Purify the flesh of the Lord," the disciples responded.

The chant grew louder as it was taken up throughout the crowd and Pastor Oagles, plunging his hands into the fire again, with sweat beading his face, roared exultantly with them, "Purify the flesh of the Lord."

He staggered back from the crucible into the arms of his disciples, apparently fainting. The crowd gasped and quietened, awaiting the next act of the drama. Oagles pushed his supporters aside and approached the podium again. He held his hands high, palms facing the crowd. He slapped his hands hard against the side of the podium. The crowd shuddered, groaned, but were stilled by Pastor Oagles's voice.

"I know no hurt. For there is no pain in the fire for those who repent. Because for them, the fire is safety from sin. I, saith the Lord, will be unto them a wall of fire round about. There is no pain in the purification of the flesh." His voice became almost a whisper. "The pain is in the knowledge of unrepented and unrepentant sin. The pain is in knowing you have offended our Lord's will and ..." He paused, then shouted accusingly, "... And do not care. For thus saith the Lord: I shall bewail many which have sinned already and have not repented of the uncleanness and fornication and lasciviousness which they have committed."

The accusing finger of Pastor Oagles shot out again at the crowd. "Be not deceived: Neither fornicators nor adulterers shall inherit the kingdom of God. You are wretches. You are fornicators. You are lewd, disgusting, lascivious sinners wallowing in the mire of your lust. Like me." He caressed his chest and repeated, his voice dropping back to a murmur, "Like me. Like me. But now ..." He paused as his hands reached upwards, palms outwards, and he swayed from side to side. "But now ..." His voice swelled as he proclaimed, "I have been purified in the fire of my Lord. I have purified the flesh of the Lord."

Many in the crowd also raised their hands and mirrored the sway of Pastor Oagles. The chant started again: "Purify the flesh of the Lord". It metamorphosed into a long drawn out phrase sung in rich, Romantic harmony and repeated over and over again: "Purify the flesh of the Lord. Purify the flesh of the Lord." Some of the crowd, followers I recognized from the woods, began to file toward the podium where they lined up at the crucible. One by one, with each phrase sung, they plunged their hands into the fire at the word 'purify' and withdrew them at the word 'Lord'. Some wept. Some smiled serenely through the ceremony. None seemed harmed by the fire. The crowd lining up at the crucible grew longer, tailing down the steps of the tabernacle and along the sidewalk. Those who had been purified in the fire joined the singing, smiling, weeping crowd, shaking hands with believers who had already undergone the trial, embracing them, then standing with their arms around one another's shoulders. At last the final supplicant repented in the fire. The chorus rose through a final, passionate phrase, culminating in a held cadence of enthralling, thrilling beauty. At its close, Pastor Calvin Oagles held out his hands to the crowd, smiling. They reached back as if to touch his outstretched hands.

"Come, my brothers, my sisters, purified followers of the Lord. Let us discuss how we may do our Lord's bidding."

He turned and led the way into the tabernacle, the disciples and new converts following him. The doors closed behind the throng.

Chapter Nine

I received an invitation to attend a special meeting of the City Association of Business and Professional Executives. The invitation came from the secretary, Elijah Ossinger, and referred pompously to "an important decision that had to be made concerning the future of our professional organization." I had little taste for meetings of the association, for the business conducted or for the concomitant socialising, but had always tolerated them in the interests of building my legal practice.

The meeting was in the boardroom of Delap Associates. By the time I arrived at the office in the Saint John city centre and made my way upstairs to the boardroom about fifty members, all men, in suits of black, grey or navy blue, were already seated. The boardroom table had been pushed aside and chairs set out in rows facing a lectern at the front of the room. Theodore Delap, with Elijah Ossinger, met me at the door. They made a curious pair, Delap with his broad shoulders, florid complexion and slicked back hair, Ossinger with his scrawny build, pinched, pasty face and head bald but for a few strands of hair. I usually took a place near the back of the room but Delap guided me to a chair at the front.

Standing behind the lectern, he opened the meeting with a prayer and Ossinger then explained what the important decision facing the association was: "The executive committee of your organization proposes that the association be renamed the Christian Association of Business and Professional Executives."

The members applauded. I made a show of clapping. Ossinger waited for the applause to die down and continued, "May I presume, then, that there are no objections to the name change?" He looked around the room. His eyes alighted on me. "Mr. Strathearn, you belong to no particular church, I believe, and of course it is your right not to do so. Would you, from your position as, shall we say, an unaligned Christian have any objection?"

"Would the name change mean the exclusion of non-Christian business people?"

"Come now, my friend, we are not about to expel any of our colleagues, nor deny membership to anyone. But your question must be moot, for surely, my friends, we are all Christian believers here."

He appealed to his audience, who responded with applause and laughter at the implied suggestion that there might be people who did not share their beliefs. Then he turned to me again.

"Thank you, Mr. Strathearn, for reminding us of our obligation, our Christian obligation, to remain open and embracing, even as we affirm the basis for our organization. And this brings me to the second reason for our special meeting, assuming there are no objections to the proposed name change."

He paused and looked around. Stared directly at me, while others followed his gaze. I looked down.

"And that is the formation of a new sub-committee of our association, the Ethical and Moral Sub-Committee."

The members applauded and when I saw several looking my way again, I joined in.

Ossinger went on, "Your executive committee has already discussed membership of this new sub-committee and proposes the following inaugural members: Mr. Delap, myself, and …" He waited again for applause to subside. "… And Mr. Strathearn."

Theodore Delap crossed the floor quickly to me, shook my hand, said, "You see, we are not an exclusive body, my boy."

I thanked my colleagues for their confidence in me. Ossinger joined us and as the three of us stood before the meeting, Delap announced, "The sub-committee has already discussed two basic—ah—moral precepts to which they invite all members to subscribe."

Turning to me, he said, "You will forgive our expediency, Mr. Strathearn, in discussing these precepts in your absence but I know you will have no disagreement with them."

Turning back to the meeting, he went on, "First, we, as an association, believe in working together for the betterment of our professional colleagues."

There was a chorus of, "We believe", in which I joined.

"Second, we, as an association, believe in the renunciation of any and all relationships deemed by the Ethical and Moral Sub-Committee to be detrimental to personal and professional morality, and to reflect badly on the association."

Again, the chorus of, "We believe", after which the meeting fell into a prayer, led by Delap. As the members bowed their heads and closed their eyes, I slipped quietly away.

Chapter Ten

It was a frigid Monday morning in January of 1935. Jenny and I were walking up from the cabins, holding hands to steady ourselves as we picked our way through the snow, when one of the mill trucks, Sonny at the wheel, skidded to a stop in front of the boarding house. Sonny jumped from the cab and ran up the steps shouting, "He went under the saw. Lamarre went under the saw." He opened the door and shouted again, "Lamarre went under the saw. Nurse, come quick."

Nurse flew out of the door and down the steps, clutching her emergency kit. She called to us, "Jenny, Duncan, come and help."

As we bounced back toward the highway, Sonny said, "He was walking beside the saw, and he slipped, and his foot went in the sawdust pit. He should have just stayed put where he was 'til we got the blade shut off but he tried to get his foot back and the blade went through his boot and near took his foot off."

We found the woods workers clustered around Lamarre, swinging their arms and stamping their feet to keep warm. Their breath hung in clouds. Lamarre lay in the snow, his eyes closed, his injured foot raised on a log. Only a thin strip of flesh held it to the rest of his leg. The snow under it was bright red. Nurse and Jenny looked at each other. Jenny raised her eyebrows. Nurse gave a slight shake of her head. The men around Lamarre caught the silent exchange and in their turn exchanged glances, shaking their heads, as if Nurse and Jenny had just confirmed what they feared.

Lamarre opened his eyes. "Hi, Nurse, Jenny. Look what I've done." Jenny felt his pulse while Nurse looked at the wound. "Fix me up, Nurse, will you, please? Can you?"

Nurse said, "I will try." She looked at Jenny. "Pulse?"

"Not bad."

"Let's stop the bleeding." She looked up at the men standing around and asked, "A scarf?" One of the men pulled off his scarf and passed it to her. She wound it around Lamarre's leg above the wound. "Something to tighten it with," she said, looking up again.

I picked up a thick wood chip. "How's this?"

Nurse took it and wound the scarf around it. Lamarre groaned. Jenny stroked his hair from his forehead. Nurse turned the wood chip three times and said, "I need a good knot." All the men moved forward. "You," said Nurse, pointing at the owner of the scarf.

He knelt and tied it, saying, "Just pull here when you want it undone."

Nurse looked at Lamarre. "Take a deep breath. We are going to move your leg."

Lamarre nodded. He breathed in and closed his eyes. Jenny stood, went to move around the injured man, and slipped in the snow. Two of the loggers caught her as she fell toward Lamarre and supported her until she was kneeling in the snow opposite Nurse.

"I'll lift the leg. I want to hold it just so. You wrap it," Nurse ordered.

Jenny reached into the emergency kit.

"Ready?" Nurse asked.

Jenny nodded. Her white dress was red where she knelt.

Nurse lifted Lamarre's ankle from the log. He groaned and his head slumped to one side.

"Good. He's fainted. Wrap the leg—quickly. It needn't be neat because the bandage is coming off as soon as we get him to the boarding house."

Jenny began to wind the cloth around the wound.

"Lower. Right over his foot," Nurse ordered.

Jenny bound Lamarre's foot.

"Now—up to the tourniquet," Nurse said.

Jenny wound until the bandage touched the scarf.

"Now use up the roll. I don't want the foot to move."

Lamarre opened his eyes.

"Nearly done—for now," Nurse told him. She looked around at the men. "I need a stretcher."

"Sleigh. Wood sleigh," said one.

Jenny moved back as the men pulled a sleigh beside Lamarre. They tore off their jackets, threw some on the sleigh and piled others beside it. They reached down. At a nod from Nurse they slipped their arms under Lamarre. Nurse and Jenny prepared to lift his feet. Their bare hands were white with cold.

"Ready?" Nurse asked Lamarre.

He breathed in deeply again and nodded.

Nurse looked around and repeated, "Ready?"

The men nodded. I had my hands under Lamarre's head.

"Lift."

As soon as we raised Lamarre he groaned and fainted again. We laid him on the sleigh.

"Rope," said Nurse. "We need to tie him securely, especially the leg."

We raised the makeshift stretcher and Sonny wound a length of rope around it, securing Lamarre.

As the men went to cover him with the remaining jackets Nurse said, "Wait." She looked at Jenny. "I want his foot packed with snow. How?"

Jenny bit her lip, glanced into the emergency bag, and said, "Make bags with the lint." She took a roll of lint from the bag and ripped off a length. "Like this, guys," she said. She picked up a handful of snow, formed it into a ball, wrapped it and tied it. "See?"

As she tore off lengths, we packed them with snow and handed them to Nurse. She stacked them around Lamarre's ankle until it was covered.

We lifted the stretcher onto the back of Sonny's truck. The men had already laid jackets and sweaters on the floor of the truck, and now they piled yet more over Lamarre.

Nurse ordered, "Sonny, Duncan, get in the back with Lamarre. Steady the stretcher. I will drive."

Sonny said, "First, you put these on, before you lose your fingers."

He passed her a pair of gloves. Another man was already tending to Jenny. He'd thrown his gloves in the snow and was holding her bare hands between his. As soon as he released them, another removed his gloves and pulled them quickly onto Jenny's hands. She smiled her thanks as she followed Nurse into the cab.

Sonny and I did our best to hold Lamarre still as the truck bounced over the rough woods trail and onto the dirt highway. By the time we turned off towards the boarding house I had no feeling in my hands and feet and I shook with a depth of cold I had never experienced before. I pushed my discomfort away as I looked at Lamarre's unconscious form, wondering at life and work in the woods with an amputated foot. When Nurse stopped the truck, Sonny grinned and said, "Now you've got the cold inside your city bones, eh? Now you know where you belong."

He jumped from the truck and lifted one end of the sleigh. "Let's get this boy inside."

I was so cold my muscles would barely respond and I could not bend my fingers. I managed to cup my wrists under my end of the stretcher and we carried Lamarre in.

While Jenny and Colleen sat with him Nurse took me aside. "I can't do much more than stop the bleeding, although I'll stitch the foot back on and splint it, so it's not flopping around. But it will have to be amputated. I want you to call at the hospital when you're in town and warn them we'll be sending him in tomorrow. I don't want to move him until then. He's had enough for now."

She returned to Lamarre and unwrapped his wound. She cleaned the stump of the leg and the mutilated ankle, picking out pieces of splintered bone.

I drove in to Saint John and took the message to the hospital before I went to my office. That night I drove back to the boarding house. In the morning I watched with Jenny, Megan and Colleen while Nurse renewed Lamarre's bandages.

When the injured foot was revealed, Nurse inspected it and said, "Well, the wound is closed." She looked more closely. "And the skin looks pink and healthy. But I want Sonny and Colleen to take you into the hospital when I have it bandaged again, to get it checked out," she told Lamarre, catching my eye briefly.

When they returned that night, they entered the crowded dining room grinning broadly. Lamarre was on crutches.

"I have a message from the doctor," he announced. "There's nothing for him to do."

"But I thought ..." Nurse started, and faltered.

"You thought I was going to lose it. He told me. You could have let me in on that. I could have handled it. But he says you did an exemplary job, as usual. Exemplary, that's what he said. That's good, isn't it?"

"It is nice of him, to say that," Nurse acknowledged.

"And he said the ankle will probably never work, but at least I'll keep my foot, and I'll be able to walk on it, likely."

While we all cheered, he hugged Nurse and asked, "What do you charge for saving a foot?"

"I'll settle for a slab of moose meat and some entertainment. Give us one of your songs," Nurse suggested.

Lamarre hobbled to the centre of the room, reached into an inner pocket and brought out his harmonica. He played the same mournful introduction as once before, then began to sing:

> *The lad from the northern isles*
> *With salt on his lips*
> *And spray on his cheek*
> *And sea in his eyes*
> *Embraced his inevitable destiny*

As father before to fish with his father
Loved the salt and the spray and the sea

The diners applauded. Lamarre repeated the introduction as a bridge between verses. I took Jenny's hand, moved by the song, and by the warmth of her body as she sat close to me, to anticipate bed and breakfast with her that night. Lamarre resumed singing:

The lad from the northern isles
With passion on lips
And blush on his cheek
And love in his eyes
Pursued the girl of his childhood
As husband intent to settle with wife
As generations before to stay in the isles
With the salt and the spray and the sea

"Musician man, sing that song," Colleen said quietly, gazing at Lamarre.

The girl from the northern isles
With curse on her lips
And rage in her cheek
Forsook her home in the isles
Adventure to seek rejecting her home
And the salt and the spray and the sea

Jenny started to cry. I squeezed her hand as Lamarre improvised a variation on the bridge, then sang on:

He came to the southern woods
With dust on his lips
And sweat on his cheek
But sea in his eyes
Accepted his inevitable destiny
As lover now to forsake for his love
The salt and the spray and the sea

Lamarre reprieved the bridge yet again, then stopped. "I can't remember the end. How does it go?"

Jenny murmured, "He died in the southern woods."

Lamarre nodded and sang:

He died in the southern woods
With blood on his lips
And gash in his chest
But sea in his eyes
She mourned the death of her love
Who dreamed boats and islands and fish
But died in the woods, far from
The salt and the spray and the sea

Jenny was still crying as we walked across the meadow to her cabin.

"What's the matter?" I asked, putting my arm around her and drawing her close, inviting her confidences as a prelude to intimacy.

"That song …"

"Yes."

"It's special for me, kind of."

"Why special?" It was special for me, too. It was the song Lamarre had sung on my first night at the Seashore Boarding House, when Jenny and I had met.

"It brings back memories."

"Ah."

Yes. The song recalled that night for her, too.

"It reminds me of someone."

She was being coy. Perhaps she wanted to talk of love, at last, and was leading to it obliquely. I prompted, "Someone you ... love?"

"Loved."

It was as if she had dashed cold water on my face. I whispered, "Loved?"

"A boy I loved."

Desire sluiced out of me in a bitter torrent. I took my arm from her waist and thrust my hands into my pockets. "A teenage love affair? Some adolescent crush?"

"A boy I loved, who died because of me."

She ran ahead of me to the cabin and went inside, leaving the door open. I followed slowly, not knowing whether to leave her to her grief or to risk intruding on it. I stopped at the cabin. Through the open door I could see Jenny lying on her bed, weeping, her face in her hands. I went in and sat beside her, my affections as desolate in their rebuff and in their inability to reach her to comfort her as hers were in their savage grief. I put out my hand to stroke her hair but withdrew it before it touched. I moved away and sat by the stove. Eventually she calmed a little.

I asked, "Is that why you'll never talk about love?"

She nodded.

"How did this boy die because of you?"

"We were childhood friends—girl friend and boy friend, you know—on the island up north where we were born. When I left and came south—there was no work up there, and my parents wanted me out—he followed me. He gave up the fishing he loved and followed me. He worked in the woods around here, to be near me. He begged me to marry him and go back to the island, and he'd go back to the fishing, and I wouldn't have to worry about finding work, but I didn't want to go back. I was independent with Nurse taking me on here."

She paused, sniffed, wiped her nose.

I'd often wondered how she arrived at the boarding house, and as if reading my thoughts Jenny went on, "Before that I was penniless, just wandering from job to job. Then I wandered out here. Well, I didn't wander here. I was hitching a ride to Saint John, hoping to find work there, and a truck driver gave me a ride and he thought I'd do him a trick in return. When I said no—it was before I got into doing the tricks—he put me out by the road in the woods and left me there. It was near the boarding house, but I didn't know that, not until Nurse came along and found me and took me in. She said I could work at the boarding house, helping with the suppers and the boarders. Then …"

"Then you started doing other work, like Megan did."

"That's right. And I was independent at last. But when he followed me here, the boy friend, of course he didn't like it, no more than you do." She managed a smile. "And one day we had a big argument over it, and so I told him I wouldn't see him again."

"You had that right."

"I suppose. But then they carried him here one day, his chest gouged out where he'd fallen on a peavey. He really shouldn't have worked in the woods. He was clumsy there, and he was so sure footed on the boats. Nurse tried to save him, but he'd lost so much blood before they even got him here. He said, 'Carry me down to the shore, boys, so I can imagine I'm home where I should be.' They took him down to the shore and laid him there, near the rocks where we like to sit. He said—they told me he said—'Just like being back home, boys.' But he wouldn't see me. He wouldn't even let me help Nurse, he was that mad at me. He died on the shore. And I did love him, you know, even if I wouldn't marry him and go with him like he wanted."

"And now you won't love anyone again, let alone marry."

"I guess."

She rose and crossed the room to me. She rested one hand briefly on my shoulder, said, "Sorry, Duncan." She stood beside me, biting her lip, her head tilted to one side. I wondered whether she wanted me to embrace her, but before I could decide she returned to the bed and flung herself down again. She cried some more until at last she slept. I covered her, then tiptoed out and went down to the shore where Jenny's childhood beau had died.

Megan was sitting on the rocks, gazing at the sea. She made room for me beside her, asking, "Are you okay, honey?" She had seen us leave the dining room.

"You knew the story," I accused.

She nodded.

"Why didn't anyone tell me?"

"It was for Jenny to tell, honey, if and when she wanted. You know that."

I sat beside her and she put her arm around me, pulling my head down to her shoulder.

"I've known Jenny nearly ten years now," she said. "And I can tell you that after the accident, and until you came on the scene, she showed no emotion at all. Now—well, she may not say she loves you, but in her way, she does."

"So I should be satisfied with an unspoken love? I have to be content with imagining someone loves me?"

Megan smiled and returned her gaze to the dark sea. "It's more than most of us can expect, honey."

Chapter Eleven

Carmen Burns came to my office in Saint John. He was a small man whose delicate features were offset by a crooked nose, crooked because it had been broken, twice, in the course of his work. He took his job and himself very seriously, even dressing in the manner he imagined a private investigator should dress, in a long raincoat, with collar turned up, and carefully angled fedora. I liked him for his integrity and for the thoroughness with which he undertook his work.

He asked, "Are you still interested in that Pastor Calvin Oagles?"

"Do you have something to add to your investigation?"

"Only what I've been hearing around the city. I got interested in him after doing the investigation for you. Last week—did you hear? —his crowd, the ones who call themselves the disciples, got a majority on the city council in the elections. Now they've got the police harassing those poor girls down by the docks—you know the ones I mean."

"The prostitutes."

I thought of Maud and Mandy, hanging over their stable door, propositioning me, then too proud to accept my offer of money without their services rendered.

"Lost souls trying to make a living, I call them."

"The police, the whole city, have known about them for years. The police have always just left them alone."

"Not any more. They've got orders to clean them out, 'to make the docks a fit place for a city which values the family above all'. That's what the council instructions to the police say. I was talking to some of the boys at the Water Street station this morning and they're not happy about it. They've always got along okay with the girls, even kept an eye out for them."

"And now they're to be driven out of the city."

"Not just them. Some of the businesses are likely to be driven out too. The Saint John Beacon's come out in support of Oagles—not surprising, the publisher and the editor are both at that tabernacle twice a week—and now they're going to print a list every week of all the businesses whose owners go to the tabernacle. And the disciples, so called, are supposed to use only those businesses. So if you've got a shop, and you're not a so called Disciple of Fire, you're likely going to lose several hundred customers. And that's a conservative estimate. It's probably more like a couple of thousand now subscribing to the tabernacle. And how long can you carry on a business like that in a city this size?

"And I'll tell you something else. Oagles—he's going crazy. I don't know who else realizes it, but that's the way he's going."

"I've always known he was a little strange. Dangerously strange."

"It's different now. Have you seen him lately? You know how he always dressed in black but with a bit of red somewhere? Well the red was getting to be more and more ..."

"I noticed that."

"... And now it's half and half red and black. Red jacket, red shirt, red tie. Black trousers. Oh—and red shoes. You'd think his followers would laugh at him, but they love it. And they're starting to dress like it too. At the tabernacle it's all red and black, they say. You know what he says? In his sermon on the radio last night ..."

"You listen to his sermons? Is this research, or ... You aren't thinking of joining him, are you?"

"The wife likes to listen to him. I'm afraid she'll start going to that tabernacle. She's a good girl, but she's always been susceptible to a smooth talker, politicians asking her to vote for them, or someone at the door wanting to sell her something. She bought two vacuums within the month once." He paused to laugh, shaking his head. "You have to love 'em, wives, don't you? They drive you crazy but you have to love 'em. And she's a good girl."

It was the longest speech I'd ever heard from Carmen Burns on any subject other than work. I found it hard to imagine him in a domestic setting, never having seen him anywhere but in my office and in court giving evidence on behalf of various of my clients. I didn't even know he was married. It was strange to hear him expressing a personal rather than a professional concern for another person.

"Maybe that's why she fell for you."

"Eh?"

"You said she's always been susceptible to a smooth talker."

"Oh. Huh. Anyway," he went on, clearing his throat as if embarrassed at his personal revelations, and resuming his professional tone, "… The wife, she was listening last night, and he says the red is for the fire in his heart which yearns for the purification of all our sins, and the black is for the blackness of all those sins, and on the day he can dress all in red, he says, that will be the day when he'll—let's see, how did he put it, I wrote in down in my notebook—here it is—'he will feel himself wholly consumed by his Lord's purifying fire, which will free him from merely condemning sin and allow him to unleash his anger and abhorrence in punitive action.' Punitive action. That's what he said. It scared me. That's why I wrote it down, to remember it."

I thanked him for the information and as he left, ventured, "Give my regards to the wife."

With Carmen Burns's warning in mind, I tuned in to Pastor Oagles's weekly radio sermon that night. He was denouncing "those who would succour the followers of Satan" when I found the wavelength.

He went on, "There are those among you, listening now, who transgress the ways of our Lord not so much by the sins you commit yourselves, of which you can always repent, but by actively helping those who deliberately set out to subvert our way of life, the way founded on our Lord's desire that we should be chaste outside His blessed partnerships, that we should turn away from the carnal desires and temptations placed before us by Satan, that we should embrace the wholesomeness of our families.

"We are cleansing our streets of the scourge of harlots and whores. Now let us look further afield. Your fathers and brothers and sons are still exposed to the temptations of the flesh by an institution not so far from here. It may not be situated within our righteous city, but it remains a temptation to the dwellers here. It has to close. Its inhabitants and its clients and its supporters have to be brought to the bosom of our family. They must be purified, or some day, their sins will burn, even as Sodom and Gomorrha, and the cities about them in like manner, giving themselves over to fornication, and going after strange flesh, are set forth for an example, suffering the vengeance of eternal fire.

"Let us start with its supporters. Do you know of someone who cavorts in its filth, who indulges his sordid appetite there? Denounce him to his family, his employer, his fellow workers, and let their scorn and derision—our scorn and derision—shame him into repentance and bring him to the welcome purification of the fire. For this ye know: Whoremongers and adulterers God will judge.

"Do you know of someone who serves this establishment? Who provides its food and maintenance and legal services? Denounce them! Tell them either to refuse it service, or to do without the support of the believing throng of the family of the tabernacle."

I turned the radio off as the disciples launched into the hymn, *My Lord is a Purveyor of Fire*. Their music had been seductively melodious when their movement was in its early stages, but as their numbers and the obduracy of their belief grew, it had become hard and nasal in a style peculiar to them, and was no longer so much music of worship as of threat.

It had grown dark while I listened to Oagles's sermon and from my apartment window I looked out over the roofs and chimneys of the city to the blackness of the woods beyond, where my friends worked, unaware of the gathering threat of Pastor Oagles and his followers. I chafed with frustration at our helplessness in the face of their taunts and threats and at Oagles's contemptuous denunciation of Nurse and the girls. And of course I wanted to defend Jenny, even as a part of me willed her to forsake her prostitution just as ardently as Oagles preached it.

Too agitated to settle to anything, I went out for a walk. I strolled through the deserted city centre and stopped at Katy's Kitchen for a cup of tea. Then I walked on and found myself at the end of Horsefield Lane. I stood in the shadows and watched the women at work in the street, some leaning over their stable doors, some strutting on the sidewalk. As I watched, two police cars pulled up, one at each end of the street. Half a dozen police constables began herding the women into the cars. I heard one say, "Sorry, darling, it's orders," and another, "This grieves me, dear, but we got no choice." As the car nearest me pulled away, the rear seat crammed with the women from the street, its headlights picked out Maud and Mandy, trying to hide in a basement stairwell. I ran to them as the car stopped and a young constable got out.

"These ladies are with me, officer," I said, as confidently as I could. "They were frightened by the arrests and couldn't bear to watch, so they tried to avoid the scene by concealing themselves. I'll look after them now, thank you."

I held out my arm to Maud and Mandy and, taking my cue, they fluttered around me, feigning nervousness. The police constable assessed the credibility accorded by my suit and by my confident manner, and retreated to his car. I led the women to Katy's Kitchen and sat them down at a table while they decided what to do.

Katy immediately appeared and ordered, "Girls, in the kitchen, quick. The police will be back."

I gave them all the money I had in my wallet, and said, "Get the first bus out of town. Go as far as you can. The city is determined to drive you out."

Mandy said, "There's a place out in the woods I've heard of, a boarding house, where some girls work. It's run by someone called Nurse. We could go there and work. We'd be safe out of the city."

"It's not far enough," I said.

They looked at me curiously and I repeated, "It's not far enough. There's danger there too. You must go further."

Maud sidled up to me and took my arm. "What can we do for you, to say thank you?"

"Not necessary."

"We could do a trick, a quick one. There's time. Katy has a room. The three of us together, you and me and Mandy, if you like. No charge. You've been that good to us."

"No. Really—no. That's not necessary. But there is one thing you might help me with."

"What's that, dear?"

"You can tell me—what would make you give up your work? I mean voluntarily, not because of some self-righteous persecutors."

The women fell silent, thinking.

Finally, Maud said, "A load of money, that'd do it. How about you, Mandy?"

"Money'd help. But what would be even better would be—a man who'd take care of me and, you know ..." Blushing through her rouge, and gazing wistfully and suggestively at me, she finished, "... And love me."

"Yeah. Some chance," said Maud.

I shook my head. "That's not enough—for at least one woman I know."

They looked at me curiously again. I wished them luck and left them with Katy, who promised to hide them until they caught the next bus to anywhere far from the city. As I walked back to my apartment, mist was moving up from the harbour, curling through the streets toward the centre and snaking out over the forest like tendrils of hate.

Chapter Twelve

It was the fall of 1936. A week of ferocious gales had caused very high tides and as I drove out of Saint John one afternoon I felt the wind roaring in from the sea. A hitchhiker, head bowed against the storm, was standing by the road. I stopped beside him.

"Where are you going?" he shouted into the wind.

"I'm going as far as the Seashore Boarding House. You can get a ride from there on into St. Stephen," I said, assuming that was his destination.

"The boarding house will do just fine," the hitchhiker said with a sly smile.

He was about eighteen, and there was something familiar about his lean face and sullen mouth. Catching me looking at him, the hitchhiker said, "Is something the matter?"

"Not at all. It's just that I feel I've seen you before. Maybe around the city? Do you live here?"

The hitchhiker ignored the question and we drove in silence until he asked, "Do you have business at the boarding house?"

"I stay there sometimes."

"You may find some excitement there this evening, according to the stories going around the city."

"What do you mean? I've heard nothing. What stories?"

The sly smile again. "You'll see."

I resisted the temptation to leave him by the road for his rudeness and again we travelled in silence. About half a mile from the boarding house a truck loaded with woods workers roared from one of the woods roads and pulled up abruptly in front of us. Sonny was driving.

"Wait here," he called to me. "More men coming. Bring them."

"What's going on?" I shouted.

"They're going to burn ..."

The rest of Sonny's words were caught by the wind and lost as the truck roared away in a swirl of dust.

"What did he say?" I asked my companion, but all I got was the sly smile yet again.

Four men ran from the woods, one of them Lamarre, limping.

I shouted, "Get in. Tell me what's happening."

"They're going to burn the boarding house," Lamarre gasped, fighting to catch his breath after the run from the woods. "One of the truckers heard the rumour in town and stopped to warn us."

"Who's going to burn the boarding house?"

"Pastor Oagles and his mob. They've got a convoy coming out. They're going to block the road both sides of the boarding house while they burn it."

As he spoke I had to brake hard as I came up against Sonny's vehicle, abandoned. In front of it a large truck blocked the road.

We ran forward. A melee of men rushed toward the boarding house, loggers coming in from the woods and mill workers who had run the two miles from the mill as the word spread. The wind was hard in our faces. It sounded the alarm on the Bear Pots by itself and drove dust and smoke into our eyes. Charlie directed the fire fighting. A chain of workers passed buckets from the sea and across the meadow.

Nurse and Jenny worked in the middle of the line. Colleen and Megan were on the shore. They plunged into the burgeoning surf. Filled their buckets. Ran back across the shingle to start them up the line. At the other end of the chain, Sonny and Randy had stripped to the waist. They received the buckets two at a time. Ran to the worst of the flames. Hurled the water on them. Ran back for more.

"Keep 'em coming, m'darlings," Randy shouted between each trip.

Even from a distance I could see the sweat dripping from his face. It streaked the soot on his huge chest and belly. His normally lustrous hair hung lank down his back.

Beside him, Sonny worked with the quiet, resigned intensity of the maritimer, schooled in the endurance of natural disaster, expecting it, coping with it, soldiering through it.

Down on the shore the roaring waves drenched Megan and Colleen. They struggled to move against their clinging white dresses. Barely pausing in their work, they tore them off and scrambled between surf and meadow in their underclothes. The dresses, flung aside, with the red sashes crumpled and wound among the sodden material, lay on the rocks like patches of bloodstained snow. On the far rocks, the seals roused themselves from their afternoon torpor and raised their heads to watch the human antics.

As I joined the chain of men, I glimpsed my hitchhiker, standing at the side of the boarding house.

"We need all the help we can get. Grab a bucket. Join the line," I shouted.

He seemed not to hear but stood, as if transfixed, watching the fire and smiling.

Despite our efforts, the flames, whipped by the wind, were spreading. I heard Jenny, from the middle of the line, call, "The cabins—they're on fire."

Charlie shouted, "Lamarre, take care of huts, look after cabins."

Lamarre took two of the men. He limped after them as they tore spruce boughs from the trees and beat at the flames that licked around the beams supporting the cabins.

With the links in the chain between shore and boarding house made even wider, the carriers began to slow as they tired. Two of the older men from the mill sank to their knees and Nurse abandoned the line to tend them. Jenny, grim and silent, covered Nurse's ground as well as her own.

At the end of the track from the highway red and black-clad figures appeared, chanting triumphantly above the roar of wind and crackle of flames.

"Lord's ire ignites the fire."

Pastor Oagles, at their head, pronounced, "Then the Lord rained upon Sodom and upon Gomorrha brimstone and fire from the Lord out of Heaven, and, lo, the smoke of the country went up as the smoke of a furnace."

Amazed by their insouciance, we paused to stare. Sonny threw aside his bucket and set off toward them, as silent and intense as when tackling the fire. He tore out one of the veranda rails for a cudgel and slammed it into his palm as he stalked forward. Several of the mill workers followed him.

Charlie shouted, "Ignore bastards, disregard blackguards. Get fire, fight flames."

Sonny looked from the disciples to Charlie. Glared back at the disciples. Raised a pointing, threatening, finger. Went back to his post. The mill workers followed his lead.

The disciples, as immaculate in their discipline as in their dress, stared impassively at us, not moving until a horn blared behind them. The Count's wagon swerved through their ranks, bounced up the dirt track and stopped.

The Count leaped from the car and announced, "Nurse, Charlie, friends, let's get this confounded fire—excuse my fulmination—under control."

Clutching his homburg to his head, his morning coat tails flying behind him, he ran to join the line near the shore, galvanizing us back into action.

A sudden huge wave clutched at Colleen as she scooped in the shallows. It dragged her into the surf. Megan screamed and ran through the water to her. She grabbed Colleen's hand. Another monstrous wave broke over them, tumbling them apart. Megan stumbled into the shallows. She screamed again as she looked back and saw Colleen struggling against the retreating surf. The men near the shore formed a new chain. They dragged Colleen on her back, spluttering and coughing, through the weedy rocks on the shore. The retreating surf grabbed, sucked at and stripped off Colleen's petticoat. She scrambled to her feet and shouted at the surf, "You can take my undies but you're not taking me, damn it," and turning on her gaping, sodden rescuers, added, "What are you looking at, you horny bastards? Let's get back to work."

She grabbed her bucket and filled it. Megan followed suit and the line resumed. As I reached for the first bucket to get to me, I looked down the line and caught Jenny's eye. She briefly shook her head in despair. Beside the line, Nurse still bent over the exhausted older men. Randy, waiting for the chain to resume, stooped with his hands on his knees, breathing heavily. Beside him Sonny squatted on his haunches, head down, shoulders heaving.

I thought, despair is overrunning us, as surely as fire will overrun the Seashore Boarding House.

Looking down to the cabins I saw Lamarre and his men flailing desperately at the flames. One of the boughs caught fire and as Lamarre flung it aside it set fire to the brush. The men abandoned the cabins and stamped on the burning foliage. Lamarre's pants leg caught fire and he limped to the sea to douse it.

Charlie, seeing him, shouted, "Lamarre. All right? Okay?"

Lamarre gave a brief wave and returned to stamping on the brush.

Charlie was close to me and caught my eye. "Hopeless. Futile," he said, as quietly as I ever heard him speak.

At the same time the wind redoubled its rage and with it the surge of the sea. Megan and Colleen, and the men near the shore, scrambled for safety as the surf surged ever higher. The waves hit the line of rocks between the beach and the meadow and sent spectacular sheets of spray into the air. The wind caught the spray and hurled it onward. The water gatherers on the shore retreated from the waves and scrambled up to the safety of the meadow. We stood in awe as again and again the waves crashed, the spray hurled, and the wind caught it and filled the air with it. Slowly the fires on the veranda and in the cabins gave way under the persistent, soaking drizzle blowing up from the sea, and the clanging of the Bear Pots was suddenly no longer alarm, but celebration.

The trail across the meadows where the chain had worked was a muddy morass. Colleen and Megan, scrambling up the bank from the shore to safety, fell twice, then crawled through the mud. Megan rose, mud covered, and shrieked with childish glee. The girls cavorted in the clean grass beside the trail as the spray washed their underclothes and their bodies clean. The Count, who had fallen into the mud as he gave his hand to try and help the girls, sadly surveyed his bedraggled morning suit, then cast it off and danced in his long johns with Megan and Colleen, still clutching his homburg to his head.

Lamarre, hobbling up from the cabins, from somewhere produced his harmonica and played a jaunty tune. He stopped playing and extemporized words:

> *I'll sing you a verse*
> *About the girls and Nurse*
> *They thought they'd burn 'em*
> *But I guess we learned 'em.*

The men took up the verse in a triumphant, riotous chorus. Alternately playing and singing, Lamarre hopped around in a frenzied dance in which the rest of the ragged believers joined. Nurse helped her patients to their feet and holding hands they danced in a ring. Jenny and the Count, and Colleen and Megan executed a wild two step, while Sonny and Randy linked arms and swung each other around.

I dropped my bucket and wiped the spray and drizzle from my eyes. My suit was muddy and sodden, and torn in two places where the buckets had snagged it. Surveying the scene, I thought, what a disheveled, motley group of comrades we are. Ragged believers, indeed. How I love you all.

I held my arms wide, looked up to the sky, and felt the sea spray stream down my face. I let myself fall slowly backwards into the long grass of the meadow. As I fell, I caught a glimpse of the disciples. They had been standing in an immaculate, astonished group, watching our antics. Now, led by Oagles, they turned and resumed their chant as they marched in procession toward the highway: "Lord's ire ignites the fire. You will learn—or prepare to burn."

The hitchhiker marched and chanted with them.

Their invocation arrested Lamarre's music and our singing and dancing. We watched their departure until we heard the roar of vehicles racing away out on the highway. Still we stood, the spray still falling, only the still sounding Bear Pots breaking the silence.

Jenny ran to me, flung her arms around me.

"I'm so frightened," she said.

Chapter Thirteen

I was drawn yet again to the tabernacle. It was the night of the weekly outdoor sermon, broadcast live on the city radio station. People were gathering before the steps half an hour before the sermon was due to begin and by the time the doors of the tabernacle burst open a large crowd was on the sidewalk and spilling into the road. The purifying fire was already in place, burning low in the crucible. At the boarding house we had been plotting the growing eccentricity of Pastor Oagles by the increasing amount of red he wore and this evening, mindful of what Carmen Burns had told me, I was convinced he had become mad. When the doors burst open to reveal him, he was clad entirely in red. He strode to the podium and waited for the excited hum that had greeted his appearance to die down. He was flanked by the most faithful of his disciples. Without surprise, I noticed among them Theodore Delap and the chief of police. I'd complained fruitlessly and uselessly to the police chief after the attempted burning of the boarding house.

A tense silence fell on the crowd as Pastor Oagles grimly surveyed them, hands on hips, shaking his head as if in disgust and despair. He flapped a dismissive hand in their direction, turned away, seemed to change his mind, as if deciding, against his better judgement, to tackle a hopeless situation, turned back to the crowd and intoned quietly, "Be not deceived; neither fornicators nor adulterers shall inherit the kingdom of God." Suddenly, both hands pointing at the crowd, embracing them all in his disgust, he cried, "You are filth. You are scum. You offend me. You revolt me. The rank odour of your licentiousness sears my nostrils. The foul taste of your debauchery sickens my tongue. My gorge rises at the lewd, disgusting depravity of your lives."

I looked around expecting to see anger at the insults, but instead saw supplicant nodding of heads, faces beseeching more degradation. Then his anger seemed to abate and he collapsed on his knees. The disciples rushed forward to support him and adjusted the microphone to his new level. Pastor Oagles was crying, real tears coursing down his face, and he was muttering, at first inaudibly, his words indistinct as he sobbed. Then I made out: "I have tried. My purifying Lord, I have tried. Forgive my failure. I have tried."

Now I sensed embarrassment among the crowd, as if they were over-hearing a private conversation and were unable to get away.

He went on, "I have begged them to renounce their sinful habits. I have ordered them to forgo their evil ways. I have even—forgive me—threatened them with your divine retribution if they would not forsake their evil. But they reject my pleas and orders and threats. Now I am un-worthy even to kneel before you and confess my failure. I am unworthy to come before these people, who come for cure of their frailty and find only my own frailty allowing them to continue. I am unworthy. I am unworthy. I am unworthy."

He beat his head on the cement step before him as he repeated, "I am unworthy. I am unworthy."

As his face appeared momentarily between blows, I could see blood beginning to ooze from his forehead and drip down his face, where it min-gled with the tears that continued as he moaned, "I am unworthy. I am unworthy."

People rushed forward to stop the self mutilation but were restrained by the disciples, who said, "Let him make his peace."

Pastor Oagles's head stayed down. The crowd fell silent. Then, "What do I hear?" he whispered.

There was no response from the crowd.

"What do I hear?" he muttered again.

There were scattered, tentative shouts of, "You are worthy," and, "Stop", which seemed to give him some strength while still not providing the means of his full recovery. Then someone, I guessed a disciple planted in the crowd for this purpose, called, "It is we who are unworthy," and fell to his knees.

The crowd rippled into similar action. "We are unworthy" rose in a huge chant. Some people beat their head on the sidewalk in imitation of Pastor Oagles, who rose, his face still bloody, but joyful now.

"What do I hear?" he called.

"We are unworthy," the crowd responded.

"What do I hear?" he roared.

"We are unworthy," the crowd roared back.

A disciple shouted, "We must be purified."

"What do I hear?" Pastor Oagles called again.

"We must be purified," the crowd responded.

"Tell me what our Lord would have us do."

"We must be purified."

"Stand and tell me, my people, what we must do."

The crowd rose and chanted, "We must be purified."

Pastor Oagles held up his hand for silence. The crowd obeyed. He nodded and smiled. He wiped tears and blood from his eyes.

"I was filth too," he murmured.

His hand upraised stilled scattered shouts of, "No," and, "We are filth, not you."

"I was scum. I cavorted in the excrement of my sin. I offended my Lord. I offended my followers. I offended myself."

The tears seemed ready to fall again. He shook himself. He murmured, "But I was saved."

The crowd murmured, "You were saved."

Oagles called, "I was saved by the fire."

The crowd chanted, "You were saved by the fire."

Oagles thundered, "I was saved by the purification of the fire."

The disciples around Oagles shouted, "Hallelujah. Bless the fire."

The crowd roared in echo, "Hallelujah. Bless the fire."

Oagles nodded and smiled at the disciples and the crowd. Tears washed down his face. The disciples formed a line each side of him. They raised their hands above their heads as they chanted, "The fire. Bless the fire. We will be purified."

The crowd, hands held high, chanted with them, "The fire. Bless the fire. We will be purified."

Oagles stepped back. He flung his arms forward, pointing at the crucible. The flames roared into a six foot blaze.

Hands held high, Oagles chanted, "Who will know the gratification of redemption in the fire?"

"The fire. Bless the fire. We will be purified," the crowd responded, hands still raised.

Oagles swayed as he chanted, "Who will know the bliss of purging sin in the fire?"

The line of disciples and the crowd swayed in unison. "The fire. Bless the fire. We will be purified."

"Who will know the rapture of absolution in the fire?"

"The fire. Bless the fire. We will be purified."

"Who will know the ecstasy of atonement in the fire?"

"The fire. Bless the fire. We will be purified."

Choral music, hard and nasal, took over the chanting. The disciples guided members of the audience up the steps of the tabernacle where they formed a line at the fiery crucible. Pastor Oagles lowered his arms. The fire dwindled back to a foot high flame at the same time.

The first in line waited at the crucible.

Pastor Oagles chanted, "Let the fire absolve your sin."

The supplicant responded, "The fire. Bless the fire. We will be purified," and plunged his hands into the flames. He withdrew them quickly. The disciples shook his hand as he joined their ranks. The next in line stepped forward. He put his hands eagerly toward the fire. Pastor Oagles held up a restraining finger.

He chanted again, "Let the fire absolve your sin."

The supplicant responded, "The fire. Bless the fire. We will be purified."

Oagles nodded and beckoned him forward. I watched as closely as I could. The supplicant thrust his hands into the fire and pulled them back quickly. I saw no sign of pain on his face. The next supplicant was already chanting his response to Pastor Oagles. I looked along the line of supplicants, which tailed down the steps into the crowd as more and more of the congregation joined it. My gaze seized on one figure on the edge of the crowd near the end of the line. Something familiar about him. Lean. Sullen. Something familiar about the stance. Watching the spectacle. Fascinated but aloof. Admiring but scornful.

On the edge of the crowd watching the spectacle.

My memory conjured him on the edge of the woods watching the spectacle.

The fire.

The stranger.

The hitchhiker.

I crossed the road and plunged into the crowd. Hands pushed me toward the end of the line. Someone said, "Take the fire, brother. Be purified. Join us," and someone else, "Praise the fire. Amen."

Now I could see my hitchhiker clearly. I followed as closely as I could as he moved forward into the crowd. His eyes were fixed on the crucible. He would have walked into people but the crowd parted for him as if he carried an aura that pushed them apart. I thought of the Red Sea rolling back for Moses.

People in the crowd spoke as they allowed him passage.

"Make way for the child."

"Bless us by taking the fire, child."

"Touch me, child, in case I don't reach the fire. Purify me."

Eyes fixed on the crucible, he moved trancelike through the crowd and along the line. He mounted the steps to its head. Those in line stood back as he passed and I heard, "Bless me, child."

"Purify me, child."

"Absolve my sins with your touch, child."

"Touch me, child."

He paused at the crucible. His eyes moved slowly from the fire to Pastor Oagles. He waited, his hands clasped before him, his eyes now cast down. Oagles, his eyes fixed on the supplicant, said nothing until Delap whispered in his ear, prompting him.

The pastor said, "Let the fire absolve your sin."

My hitchhiker, raising his eyes to the crowd, chanted, "The fire. Bless the fire. We will be purified."

He plunged his hands into the fire.

And left them there.

His face contorted. Sweat formed on his forehead. His eyes closed.

The singing stopped. The crowd fell silent. The disciples moved toward the hitchhiker but Delap held up a hand to stop them and I heard him say, "Let the child be."

Oagles watched.

The boy took his hands from the fire. He looked at them and smiled. He looked at Oagles. Turned to the silent crowd and held up his hands. They were blistered and raw.

I thought: The stranger has gone from the edge of the crowd to the forefront. No longer watching the spectacle; now he is the spectacle.

Delap whispered again to Oagles, who muttered into the microphone, "Let us all now …"

He stopped, until Delap cued him again.

"Let us all now show our belief in the power of the fire by …" Oagles looked at Delap, who whispered a few more words. Oagles went on, "…

By carrying our torches through the streets of the city … to spread our purifying force."

One of the disciples passed a cloth-bound stick to Oagles. With Delap guiding his hands, Oagles placed it in the crucible. He removed it, aflame. Delap lifted his leader's hand with the torch and looked at the crowd, cueing their roar of approval. But the eyes of the crowd were still on the child, who, with his charred hands, seized a torch from one of the disciples and plunged it into the fire.

He lifted it. Watched the fire catch and grow. Waved it high in the air. Shouted, "Let us purify the city."

The crowd cheered and repeated, "Purify the city."

The disciples guided Pastor Oagles down the steps into the crowd. Delap and the chief of police flanked the child as he followed. The congregation pushed past Oagles and the disciples to get closer to the child, then fell back when he reached the foot of the steps. The child, still with Delap and the chief of police, moved forward past Oagles, the crowd parting for them. The eyes of the congregation feasted on the burned hands of the child.

As he strode forward he repeated the chant, "Purify the city."

The crowd took it up. "Purify the city."

The child paused on the edge of the crowd and waited for Oagles and the disciples to catch up. He stepped back so that Oagles could take his place at the head of the procession. The crowd formed into a snaking column behind Oagles as he led the procession toward the city centre.

Chanting, "Purify the city," he looked back at the congregation and at his disciples.

But their eyes were on the child.

Chapter Fourteen

Carmen Burns, haggard faced, came to my office again. He held his fedora in one hand, a sheaf of hand written papers in the other.

He said carefully, laying the papers on my desk, "Here's a final report on your friends at the tabernacle. You get this one for nothing because I did it for myself. I wanted to understand what's happening around here. The wife's gone. Gone to the tabernacle. She chose it over me."

He jabbed his thumb hard at his chest as he repeated, "Over me. That tabernacle's more important to her than twenty-five years together."

He breathed deeply, shaking his head. He flung himself into the chair beside my desk and went on quietly, "So I'm moving on. I'm not staying around to be talked at by my wife's friends and laughed at by mine."

"My friend, I'm sorry. I don't know what to say."

I imagined Jenny deserting me and felt a flood of sympathy for Burns's bitterness.

"There's nothing to say, except it's ironic it was Oagles's preaching that turned her, drew her into the tabernacle like she was hypnotized, and now she's there, he's gone."

"I heard he'd retired."

"He's more than retired. He's been committed. To the mental institution. And guess who signed the committal? The new pastor, that's who. The one who stuck his hands in the fire. They're calling him the Reverend Child now. He was the only one who'd claim responsibility for old Oagles. Did you hear where they found him?"

"All I heard was that he'd retired from the tabernacle."

"He should have retired from more than that. The police raided the Harbour Lane Exercise and Massage Club—heard of it? —and found him there. Couldn't hush it up. Well, they didn't want to. They were still upset with how he'd forced the prostitutes out of business down at the docks.

The guys down at the Water Street station told me what was going on. I wrote it all down—bad, I know, it's supposed to be confidential, but I'm so upset about the wife I couldn't help myself. Pastor Oagles was on the massage table when they went in, with two young girls at work on him. He jumped up, stark naked, not even a towel around him, and said the guys— the police! —should join him. Said unless they experienced what they were prosecuting, I wrote down what they told me, "They could not root out what they did not know." Then he started singing—I wrote this down too—"We must strive to understand the unrepentant hoard, so we shed our clothes for Jesus, we are naked for the Lord." He sung it to the tune of one of their tabernacle hymns. How's that for a religious anthem? It was a scene, the guys said. Anyway, here's the scoop on the Reverend Child, the new man at the tabernacle, for your information, free. He scares me— and he should scare you, too."

He stood and pulled the raised collar of his long raincoat tight around his neck. He replaced his fedora, angling it just so, and said, "Good luck, friend. I've enjoyed working with you."

I shook his hand and wished him good luck. I took up his final report from my desk.

Thaddeus Morley, a.k.a. The Reverend Child, is truly a Man of Mystery. I can find no information on his life before his attendance at the St. Paul's Preparatory Seminary, Halifax, Nova Scotia. Parents are unknown. Childhood and early schooling are unknown. I contacted the seminary, where staff remembered Mr. Morley as a serious and highly regarded student.

The Reverend Child—I have to refer to him as such, because he has no other reference here—seems to have bypassed study at the full seminary and to have moved directly from Preparatory Graduate to a position of influence at the Tabernacle of the Disciples of Fire. Thence he has moved to the position of what they call Minister Most Superior, following the commitment of the Church's former leader.

Under the Minister Most Superior's guidance, a number of changes and developments have taken place:

The 'disciples' have adopted conservative dark suits instead of the red uniform of their former leader.

The Reverend Child has preached on the radio about the "Lord's need for cash in order that His work may be done", and cash—amount undivulged, but believed to be considerable—has flowed into the tabernacle.

City bars are being closed down after the Reverend Child's proclamation that, "When there is harmony and unity in the family, there is harmony and unity in the workplace. This promotes the honest toil so valued by our Lord. Let us shun city establishments which promote the disintegration of family life through the consumption of alcohol."

The Reverend Child is now seeking a place that will become a 'Holy Retreat'.

Two Sundays ago he also preached the following, which I quote for your especial information, Mr. Strathearn: "Let us bring to the inhabitants of a certain Sodom in our midst (meaning the Seashore Boarding House, with which, I believe, you have a connection, no disrespect intended) the blessings of our Christian way. Let us turn them to the light of our understanding. Let us lead them through the fire of redemption so that they may share our glorious state."

Respectfully submitted: Carmen Burns, Investigative Services Inc.

Chapter Fifteen

The Ethical and Moral Sub-Committee sent me notice of a special meeting at which, the notice said, 'the sub-committee will discuss how it can help members whose unfortunate choice of relationships is adversely influencing their business.' I didn't attend and the next morning Delap and Ossinger visited my office. I shook hands with them and invited them to sit.

"We had hoped to see you last night, my boy. The sub-committee was—ah—disappointed that you were unable to be there," said Delap.

I shrugged.

Ossinger said, "It was an important meeting, as you know, held with your best interests in mind."

"I'm sure my best interests were at the heart of the meeting," I put in.

"The—ah—flippant attitude and tone I detect in you, my boy, do justice neither to you, nor to the gravity of the situation in which you find yourself. We—the sub- committee, that is …"

"That is—you and Mr. Ossinger," I supplied.

"Mr. Ossinger and myself, who together represent the membership and the expressed values of our Association. We, the sub-committee, seek associates and—ah—acquaintances for you more suitable than those with whom you at present choose to consort."

"Consort? What sort of pompous, antiquated language is that? Do you mean spend time with?" I asked.

"We mean … consort," Delap intoned.

Ossinger went on, "We discussed you, in your absence …"

"I'm sure you did," I interrupted.

Delap sighed and shook his head.

Ossinger also sighed and shook his head before continuing, "… And we have a plan, one carefully formulated to enhance your business and your personal life by guiding your choice of associates, at the same time as it prevents any unfortunate choices which you will appreciate reflect badly on our business community."

Delap took over. "There are three steps outlined. First, my boy, you will give up all association with the Seashore Boarding House and its—ah—inhabitants. Second, you will be visited weekly by our Family Support Group, who will encourage you in the third step, which is that you will assume a new choice of companions."

"I've never heard of the Family Support Group. Is this another new sub-committee of the Association?"

"It's a group we've recently formed in conjunction with the Reverend Child of the Tabernacle of Fire. Our members felt that the Tabernacle and our Christian Association had so much in common that we could do much of our work together and at some point merge our respective organizations."

Delap chided gently, "You would know this if you attended our meetings. We have missed you recently."

"Will the Family Support Group provide a choice of approved companions for me?"

"Of course, if you wish. Indeed, they will be your new companions. You will find many suitable and worthy associates in the Tabernacle."

"What if I decline the services of this Family Support Group?"

"That would be—ah—a mistake, my boy."

"Let us suppose it, nevertheless."

"If you choose to decline the help of the Family Support Group, my boy, you will prove yourself unworthy to be a member of our Association. You will then be sanctioned by the Christian Association and by the Bar Association. You will be summoned before the bar—of which, I will remind you, I am president—to answer a complaint that will be laid against you. The complaint will state that your known—ah—intimacy with prostitutes and a known abortionist at the Seashore Boarding House compromises your ability to advise on the law. Both prostitution and abortion are, as you well know, crimes, which you endorse and approve by your complicity. My boy, you cannot both administer and flaunt the law at the same time."

As he spoke, Delap rose from his chair, Ossinger following him, and they advanced on my desk until they were standing over it, leaning towards me. I sat back, locked my hands behind my head, and put my feet on my desk.

Delap took a deep breath, shook his head, and went on, "Furthermore, the lease on your office will be terminated immediately by your landlord, who is, as you know, a colleague in the Association, and then you will find it difficult, I promise you, to find alternative premises."

They wished me well, asked if we could pray together, and when I refused, said they would pray for me, and left.

I worked late that night, then, still disturbed and angry at the exchange with Delap and Ossinger, on impulse drove out to the boarding house, seeking comfort with Jenny. It was dark when I arrived and I walked past the boarding house, across the meadows toward the cabins. As I approached, the door of Jenny's cabin opened and a man emerged. Finding Jenny working was a risk I took when I arrived unannounced and I was prepared for a wait. I was about to step off the trail, out of the moonlight and into the shadows, while he passed, when I recognized him.

"Sonny?"

"Duncan? Is that you? I thought you were in your city."

"I was. I came out unexpectedly."

He nodded. We looked at each other, then gazed out to sea, as if searching for something.

"It's a clear night," he said.

I nodded.

"I was with Jenny."

The breeze off the sea rippled through the aspens. We looked at them, then back at one another.

"I hope you don't mind. I usually see Megan, but she was busy, and—well—I had to, you know …"

"I know. It's business."

"That's what it is. Just business. It doesn't mean anything."

We could hear rustling in the woods behind the cabins.

"Sounds like a porcupine," he said.

"Or a raccoon."

We listened intently.

"Do you want to punch me out?" he said suddenly.

"Why would I want to do that to a friend, even if I could?"

"I thought maybe it'd make you feel better."

"I don't feel bad. I'm used to it."

"She's a good girl. I envy you, being her friend. Her special friend. You know what I mean."

He nodded, gazed once more at the invisible rustling, said again, "I envy you, Duncan," and walked on.

A match flared in Jenny's cabin and I saw her shadow as she went around lighting the lamps. She charged more for transacting business with the lamps lit. Most of the men preferred the dark, although I could never understand why, unless it was the extra money. I'd have paid extra just to look at her.

I walked down to the beach and sat on my usual waiting rock. She would know I was there. She always knew.

I resented Sonny's use of Jenny. His dismissal of it as just business almost made it worse. How could making love with Jenny be just business? I arose abruptly and walked further up the beach. At the end of the cove I climbed over the rocks and sat out of sight of the cabins.

115

I heard her footsteps on the shingle. Heard them pause at my waiting rock. Then, surely, they came on. She divined not just my presence, nor just my hiding place, but also my thoughts. I was ashamed of my anger and of my childish hiding. She climbed around from the cove and stood near me.

"You're upset because it was Sonny."

"I'm always upset when you do business."

"But you especially resent business with someone you know well, a friend."

"Yes. And I don't know why."

As she moved to sit beside me, the moonlight shone through her thin white dress, silhouetting her body. I longed for it, for her. But my resentment drove me to try and hurt her.

"Did you, you know, come?"

"You know I never do. Just with you. There's business, and there's you."

"That's what Sonny said. It was just business."

"He's right."

"How can making love with you be just business?"

"It's not making love when I'm working. I must have told you that a thousand times. With you, it's making love. When I'm working, it's doing business. In the dining room, I get paid for serving supper. In the cabin, I get paid for serving sex."

She put her hand tentatively on my shoulder. I turned away from her. She let her hand fall. We sat in silence, watching the waves lapping at the shingle. Then she rose, climbed around the rocks, and walked back up the beach. After a while I followed her. When I reached her cabin, the lights were out. I pictured her lying in the darkness in her narrow bed, all softness now, her severity spent. I pictured myself quietly entering the cabin, shedding my clothes in the darkness and silence, and going to her, to consummate my apology.

She would be waiting for me to do this.
I walked on and drove back to the city.

Chapter Sixteen

I spent the night walking the streets of Saint John. With the prostitutes driven from them and the bars closed down, it was quiet and safe. As I paced the deserted streets I reflected on my friendship with Jenny, on the mix of joy and torment it brought me. I regretted my petulant outburst and with it the loss of a night with her through my stubborn refusal to make amends. I regretted the infantile jealousy that still raged through me. I regretted the nagging doubt her refusal to declare love, her inability to feel love, left in me.

But not for a moment did I regret my friendship with her.

In the morning I attended to a few items of my dwindling business and then, with a court appearance scheduled for the following day in St. Stephen, set off for the Seashore Boarding House. About two miles from Ratters Lake I realized the slow moving cloud of dust ahead of me contained the Count's wagon. I slowed and followed, guessing he was also headed for the boarding house. Our stately pace gave me lots of time to look around and ahead where, peering through the dust, I saw a huge bull moose in the middle of the highway, apparently oblivious of the approach of both our vehicles. At the same time as I wondered whether the Count had seen it, I heard his horn start to sound and continue to blare as he headed straight for it without slowing. I braced myself for dealing with an accident, wondering whether Nurse would be home to tend to the Count's injuries, but at the last minute the moose, with a disdainful glance, moved like a sailing ship into the woods and we drove on to the boarding house.

Still shaken by the near accident, I greeted the Count with, "I didn't think the moose was going to move for you."

"I warned it I was coming. I can't be expected to sound the klaxon and apply the brake at the same time. Having been given a warning that I'm coming, the responsibility is with the animal to move."

A horse and buggy arrived behind us, driven by a woman I recognized from Hedgehog Mountain. The Count offered his hand to help her as she climbed down with a young child in her arms.

"Mrs. Hatt. How pleasant to see you."

"Hello, Count. I'll have another of those girdles next time you're up at Hedgehog Mountain."

"I'll be delighted to supply it. Would that be the Ladies' Friend or the Tummy Trimmer, Mrs. Hatt?"

"The Ladies' Friend. That's the one."

"A wise choice." The Count nodded gravely. "I don't have that particular model with me now but I'll make a point of bringing one on my next trip."

Mrs. Hatt hitched the child higher in her arms and, business completed with the Count, addressed me. "Is Nurse in?"

"I don't know. We've just arrived. What's up?"

Nurse often slept in the afternoon and I wondered whether the girls could deal with the woman to save her being disturbed. I knew the girls would be down on the rocks.

"He's plugged," the woman said, holding out the child. "He's plugged awful. He's so plugged he's swelled. I don't know what he's been eating."

I was about to walk down to the beach to fetch the girls when Nurse opened the door onto the veranda, rubbing her eyes.

"You were asleep," I said.

"I must have dozed off. How is baby Elijah, Mrs. Hatt?"

The woman repeated her diagnosis and pulled the child's clothing down to reveal a hugely swollen bottom.

"That's not constipation. That's infection," Nurse said. "I'll lance it. That'll take care of it."

"Will it hurt him?"

"Just for a moment."

"Can't you give him something?"

"I'm afraid not. A local anaesthetic will only add to the tension there already, and he's too young for a general anaesthetic. But it'll be over in a few seconds. I'll just need your help to hold him while I lance it."

"Shall I fetch one of the girls?" I asked.

"We'll be all right. Just stay close in case I need an extra pair of hands."

We went inside to a corner of the dining room where the girls always kept a table scrubbed ready for emergencies. Nurse fetched her bag. She laid the child face down on the table. The mother cushioned baby Elijah's head. The Count and I watched.

"Ready?" Nurse asked.

The mother nodded. Nurse made a quick jab into the swelling. Mother and baby screamed and a stream of pus spurted from the incision. As she squeezed the last of the poison from the wound, Nurse suddenly leaned forward, looking closely at her incision.

"How does Elijah get around?" she asked.

"Well he won't crawl yet. He scoots around on his bum."

"That explains how he picked this up then." Nurse held out a solitary oat with an arrow sharp head. "It must have embedded itself as he shuffled around on his bum. Then infection set in and it got worse and worse."

Mrs. Hatt's hands flew to her face.

"I thought he was just cranky. I spanked him when he kept crying. I spanked him—on his poor bum. Then I just thought he was plugged with something he'd found and eat." She picked up the child and stroked his back as she held him against her shoulder.

As she left, Mrs. Hatt told Nurse, "I don't have anything for you, to thank you, not today. But my husband will have some deer meat in a month or two and we'll send some up."

"You know you don't have to, but thank you."

Mrs. Hatt went on shyly, "I do have something for you now, though."

"What's that?"

"Some advice."

"On what?"

"On looking out for yourself." When Nurse said nothing, Mrs. Hatt went on, "I had a visit—we all did in Hedgehog Mountain—from that Reverend Child and his men. They were very nice. They spoke nicely. They prayed with us and told us we were blessed and precious in the Lord's sight."

"That was good of them."

"Then the Reverend Child said we weren't to come here."

Nurse again said nothing.

I asked Mrs. Hatt, "Did he say why not?"

"He said this was a place of evil because of the forniculation that went on here. And we weren't to let our menfolk come here neither."

"Not even to dine in the evening with their womenfolk?" Nurse asked.

Mrs. Hatt shook her head.

"What about bringing children who need medical treatment? Did the Reverend Child approve that?" I asked.

"I didn't say as I agreed with him," Mrs. Hatt said quickly. "I just said it to warn Nurse. Because that's not all he said. He said you were evil, Nurse, and I don't think that's right of him."

"You don't think I'm evil, then?"

"No. 'Course not. But after he'd finished talking, there's them that was beginning to think you are, excuse me for saying so, but I did say I wanted to warn you. And the Reverend Child and his men, they're coming back next week to pray with us some more."

As the horse and buggy disappeared, Nurse said, "Is it time to counter this talk somehow? Is it serious enough to be considered slander?"

"I've thought about that already. Even if we had the resources to prosecute for slander, it's unlikely we'd be successful. We'd be in a vulnerable position, with the girls and with the curing."

We went out onto the veranda. Nurse sat beside the Count, who put his arm around her and hugged her.

She reflected, "I left the city nearly twenty years ago with my name and my reputation in shreds. Since then, since I've been living here, the Seashore Boarding House has become, I truly believe, a place to come to for help and friendship. And I never deliberately set about repairing my name and my reputation but I believe that is what has happened."

"You bet it is," the Count put in.

Nurse leaned forward in her chair. "Now am I to be chased from here, my name and reputation all tattered and ragged again? Where shall I go this time? Up north somewhere? Find a boarding house in the northern woods? Start again? Then how long before the next Pastor Oagles, or Reverend Child, descends there, and decides he doesn't approve of what I do?"

She sat back again, musing, "I never planned on the boarding house being anything more than a boarding house. It just grew into a clinic and a brothel. It is a place of friendship, a place of helping, isn't it?"

The Count and I nodded. I'd never heard Nurse speak so uncertainly.

She went on, "I wasn't driven by any kind of belief to make it that way. It just happened. Perhaps I need to invent some beliefs to shout about. Then perhaps I wouldn't be so vulnerable to people who shout about theirs."

"The boarding house became what it is, the place of friendship and helping you describe, because of who you are, and the sort of person you are," said the Count.

"You don't have to preach any beliefs," I added. "You live your beliefs. We do, too, by coming here and being part of the Seashore Boarding House. The Reverend Child and his like, they make lots of noise about their beliefs, but what do you see of their living them? I know they go to the tabernacle and preach and distribute pamphlets, but that's not living their beliefs. That's not doing something with them. That's just for show."

"What about being so opposed to us? What about trying to destroy the Seashore Boarding House? Isn't that living their beliefs?" Nurse suggested.

"If that is living their beliefs, then you'll have to tell me what those beliefs are," I retorted. "Just what do they believe in?"

The Count smiled and urged, "Go on, Mr. City Lawyer."

Nurse considered and said, "They talk about the family. They say they believe in the family."

"What's the connection between believing in the family and wanting the Seashore Boarding House destroyed?" I asked.

"They think the boarding house is a threat to families, because of the girls, because of the whoring. And they don't like the curing I do here," Nurse said.

"Look at it like this," I countered. "Men come to the girls for sex, sometimes for a little comfort, too, sometimes for a kind of friendship. Now—intimacy, comfort, friendship ..." —I ticked them off on my fingers— "... that sounds a lot like the things you'd get from a family. The Seashore Boarding House doesn't destroy families. It makes a family. It is a family."

"Not what they'd call a family."

I shrugged. "A family, all the same."

"What about the curing?" the Count asked.

"The women who come here to be cured are either young girls facing disgrace because of an illegitimate birth, disgrace and probably the loss of any prospect of marriage and family life, or married women who simply can't cope with another child. Isn't that right?"

Nurse nodded assent.

I went on, "In both cases, then, curing, far from threatening the family, in fact serves to maintain it. The Seashore Boarding House serves the family, as well as creating its own family."

Nurse considered again. At last she nodded and said, "I guess."

The Count applauded and said, "The defence rests."

We sat in silence until Nurse suggested, "So my boarding house—our boarding house—is the edifice of our beliefs. It is our tabernacle."

"And that makes us …?" I said, trying to tease her out of her gloom.

"My boarders and my diners and my patients are my congregation, my believers," said Nurse, smiling.

"Your ragged believers," the Count concluded.

I left them sitting on the veranda and went to find Jenny. The girls were, as I expected, lying on the rocks. Jenny removed her red sash when she saw me.

"You two," said Megan, indicating Jenny and me.

"We were just talking about you two," said Colleen.

"What were you saying?" I asked.

"Never mind what they were saying," Jenny said, taking my arm and leading me away.

"We were saying you must really love her, to put up with her still doing the business," Megan called after us.

"And we wished we had a man to love us like that," Colleen added.

"You talked of love?" I asked Jenny, as we walked across the meadow toward her cabin.

"*They* talked about love. They're always talking about love. It's as if they think talking about it will produce it."

"I wonder where love does come from," I mused.

"From friendship, of course."

Her face was severe as she spoke about love but turning to me it softened. "I'm truly sorry I have to do my work."

"And I'm sorry I care so much about it. I'm sorry, too, for letting it show in the childish way I do, for taking out my insecurities on you."

We sat on the step of Jenny's cabin. The tide was low and waves rolled in with hardly a ripple. The seals languished on the further rocks and sandpipers skittered along the shore. A pair of blue jays caroled and chattered in the trees behind us and on the far side of the meadow, beyond the boarding house, two deer grazed. On the veranda, Nurse and the Count still sat, old friends with heads close.

Jenny said suddenly, as if reading my thoughts, which were still on Mrs. Hatt's warning, and whose turmoil clashed with the peace around us, "What will become of us all?"

In the morning when I walked up from Jenny's cabin, the Count was leaning into the back of the Hudson, arranging boxes of clothing in the order of his day's visits.

"Looks like a busy day ahead," I said.

The Count paused in his work, leaning on the vehicle and breathing heavily. "Yes, I suppose it is a busy day ahead," he said. "But every week I seem to do more visits and sell less. And look, here's the cause of the problem."

He reached into the Hudson and produced a thick catalogue, flicking through the pages to reveal everything from household items to automobile parts. "This is where people are buying from now. They don't need anyone coming around with a wagon load of goods. They can find far more in these catalogues than us travellers could ever hope to offer. It's the same with Randy. We're being put out of business by picture books."

I could find nothing to say.

The Count flung the catalogue back into the car and slammed the door. He said, "When was the last time you saw a caribou?"

"I don't think I've ever seen one. Why do you ask?"

"Because that's what Randy and me are going to be like. Twenty years ago, when they first ran the highway through these woods, there were caribou around here, not common, but you'd see them, along with the deer and the moose and the bears. Now there's hardly a caribou left in this part of the world. Well, that's Randy and me. We're like the caribou. We're disappearing. We're victims of progress." The Count climbed slowly into the driver's seat and started the engine, still talking. "They said they'd find me a place in the store down in Halifax, but I said I wanted to carry on with the sales route. They said one more year. That was three years ago.

Well, you know what they say? They say old travellers never die. Their routes just dry up. I guess that's what's happening to me. My roots are drying up."

He released the brake and the car lurched forward.

"Look out for those moose," I called.

His hand waved from the window as the wagon drove slowly and majestically out of sight towards the highway.

Chapter Seventeen

In the summer of 1937 I was living at the Seashore Boarding House, sharing Jenny's cabin and working at the mill. With Charlie's help, I had been taken on there as personnel manager and company secretary not long after I had decided to abandon my law practice rather than answer to the Bar Association's charges. In addition to defending myself I would in any case have been in search of new premises to replace those whose lease had been rescinded, true to Delap's threat. Moreover, my clients were succumbing to the Tabernacle's pressure and going elsewhere for legal help. I hated giving in to threats, but I would have hated even more having the disciples watch my discomfort.

It was late one afternoon when Sonny put his head around the door of my office at the mill. It was a dusty little room furnished with a battered wooden desk and a rickety chair. I'd quickly grown to feel at home there, although it contrasted markedly with my old law chambers.

"You know the law, eh?" said Sonny.

"Well—some. What's up?"

"I just drove past the boarding house on the way here with a load of logs. There's a crowd there, on the highway where you turn in to the boarding house. I think they're Oagles's old crowd, only they're dressed like a bunch of politicians now, all dark suits and ties and polished shoes, and with a new guy in charge, I hear. Can we move them on?"

"Not with any force of law. There's no statute that says they can't gather on the highway. Are they obstructing the road?"

"Yes and no. When I drove toward them, they were all over the highway and they weren't going to get out of my way. Then this young feller— can't have been more than a teenager ..."

"That would be the new man in charge. The Reverend Child they call him."

"Well, he just raised his hand and they lined up across the track into the boarding house. I guess they thought I was going that way and they were planning on stopping me. It bothered me, that they thought they had the right to stop me, and how they did just what they were told, like they were in the army or something. I stopped further up the highway to watch them, in case they went on up to the boarding house and tried to burn it down like before."

"I don't think they'd do something like that under their new leader."

"You may be right, because they just stood there, staring at me. I watched them for a bit, then came right on here to see what we should do. Why don't I take some of the guys and clear them out?"

"They'd just come back, and in a strange way, it's what they want, to be beset."

"And you say we can't get the law on them, either?"

"They'd be the ones with the law on their side if we cleared them out with force. The only way the law might be on our side would be if they were threatening anyone, or actually stopping anyone entering. Even then, I doubt whether the police would be interested in helping us, anyway."

"So what are they doing there?"

"Picketing, I'd guess. Trying to discourage anyone from visiting the boarding house. I'll go take a look."

Driving out of the mill road onto the highway, I could see a construction crew in the distance. The road from Saint John to St. Stephen was being paved, disturbing the peace of the woods for ever, I feared. I hadn't driven far when I encountered Megan and Colleen. They were walking beside the road, their white dresses billowing around them in the breeze. I pulled up beside them and they squeezed into the front seat with me. They told me Nurse and Jenny were at the boarding house curing a couple of girls from Wesserunsett and that they'd been out since early morning visiting some of Nurse's patients in Eagle Rock and Nepisguit. Although they'd got a ride from one community to the other, they'd also walked about ten miles during the day.

"One more stop," Megan said. "We got to pick up groceries at the store. Want to play taxi, honey?"

I drove the girls to Ratters Lake. Like all the woods communities, it was no more than a collection of a few houses, a church and a store strung along a dirt road a mile or two off the highway. The Ratters Lake Boulevard, as the villagers called it, wound a little way around Ratters Lake itself before giving way to dense woodland. The lake stretched five miles into the interior, surrounded, like the village, by softwoods and bog. The Ratters Lake store consisted of one room of the Eldridge house. One wall of the room was lined with shelves bearing tins and boxes of food, another with trestle tables laden with clothes, and another with racks of coats, jackets and dresses. The kitchen table, placed across the doorway to the kitchen, served as counter. Mrs. Eldridge, who was all watchful stillness and sudden nimble movement, like the white tailed deer which teemed in the woods, said, "Oh, dear," when we walked in.

Colleen said, "Why 'Oh, dear'?"

"I can't sell to you. Well, I will today. You've been good customers all these years, you and Nurse. But I'm afraid I can't sell to you after today."

"Why can't you sell to us?" Colleen asked.

I knew what the answer would be before Mrs. Eldridge spoke. The disciples had extended their tactics of intimidation to businesses outside the city, reaching even these little woods communities.

"Some of my customers—not many, well I don't know how many, but a few, enough to be a worry—they're saying if I sell to you, they won't come here to buy. It's hard enough to make ends meet as it is. I can't afford to lose customers."

"But you can afford to lose us, is that it?" Megan demanded.

"I don't want to let you and Nurse down. You know that. But if I keep serving you, there's more than you that won't come here for their groceries."

"And I suppose the fact that Nurse delivered your little Sam and helps Samuel Senior when he gets his coughs—that doesn't count for anything, eh? And didn't we come visiting when you had that water on your knee last fall?"

Megan was advancing on Mrs. Eldridge, her finger pointing and her voice rising as she crossed the room. Mrs. Eldridge retreated further into the kitchen.

"It's not my fault, Megan."

"Well, it sure as shit ain't my fault either, honey. So just who do you think I should blame?"

I put my hand on Megan's arm. "Megan, you know who to blame."

She kicked the nearest table and left, slamming the door.

Mrs. Eldridge gestured tiredly at her goods, saying, "Get what you want." She added, "Sorry."

Colleen and I gathered as many provisions as we could manage and paid at the kitchen table. Mrs. Eldridge's hand was shaking as she took the money.

"I guess we say goodbye then," Colleen said.

"Sorry," Mrs. Eldridge said again.

As we left she called after us, "Samuel Senior does get his coughs, like Megan said, so when he does, do you think Nurse would ...?" She paused as Colleen slammed down her box of groceries on the roof of the car and turned on her. Mrs. Eldridge finished, "I mean, what should Samuel Senior do?"

I stood in the doorway to stop Colleen going back in and said, "Colleen, let me explain to Mrs. Eldridge."

Mrs. Eldridge smiled timidly and helplessly at me.

I said, "Next time Samuel Senior gets his coughs, tell him from Nurse and the girls that he can go to hell."

As we loaded the groceries in the back seat, we noticed another boarding house patient, Mrs. Cooke, standing in front of her house across the road, watching us, arms folded. Her greying hair was pulled back severely and wound into a tight bun. Her thin lips were pursed so tightly they puckered. Her eyes, small and narrowed, darted between Colleen and Megan.

"How's the arthritis, Mrs. Cooke?" Colleen asked, climbing in beside Megan.

"Nothing I can't bear with the good Lord's help."

"I reckon that's all the help you'll be getting from now on. Don't come to us next time it's acting up. Just ask the Lord for a treatment."

Megan leaned toward the open door and called, "Will you and Mr. Cooke be dining at the boarding house tonight?" She'd been pacing beside the car while she waited for Colleen and me. I could tell she was spoiling for a fight.

"We won't be setting foot in that house until the sin is driven out," Mrs. Cooke declared.

"What sin would that be?" Megan asked.

"You know very well the sin I'm talking about. The sin that you do, you and those other … girls."

"Jealous, are you?" Megan taunted. "Not getting any yourself? I'm not surprised. Mr. Cooke doesn't usually have much energy left when he leaves us."

Colleen slammed the door.

As we drove back through the woods and onto the highway, I warned the girls about the picketers. We found them formed up in a line across the track leading down to the boarding house, a dozen disciples, as immaculate as ever in their dark suits and sober ties, but with no sign of red now. I drove as close as I dared to the line. The Reverend Child himself, my hitchhiker, stood in the centre of the line, confronting us, his arms folded.

"Run over the bugger," whispered Megan.

"Let's see what they do," I said.

The front of the car was inches from the Reverend Child. I released the brake and we jerked forward. I braked again. I was sure the hood of the car must be touching him. His only response was the sly smile I remembered from when I gave him a ride out to the boarding house.

"In the name of the Disciples of Fire, and with the authority of their executive committee, I make this formal representation to you, not to enter this place of degradation," he declared.

I backed up.

The disciples, mistaking my intentions, still in their unmoving rank, applauded.

I accelerated hard. The Reverend Child flung his arms wide and dropped his head as if impaled on a cross, at the same time moving, with the disciples, to make two ranks lining the track. I had braked hard just before this action, having no intention of injuring them. Now I edged forward again. The disciples moved close to the car, peering in at us with solemn, sorrowing faces. They sang the hymn *Forgive them their weakness, They know not how they grieve You*. Megan knelt on the seat and exposed her bum to them as we passed through.

We found Nurse and Jenny, and Mr. and Mrs. Charlie, on the veranda. Charlie said he had heard about the picketing and had come to the boarding house on one of the trails through the woods to warn Nurse.

"Protect if have to, look after if necessary," he added, nodding at his hunting rifle propped in a corner of the veranda.

The girls who had been cured were resting, said Nurse, and she was planning on sending them out through the woods trail the next day.

Jenny and I walked down to her cabin. My move to the Seashore Boarding House, to Jenny's cabin, had been the result of an almost casual exchange between us. When I told her about Delap and Ossinger's plan to have me evicted from my office, she said, "Next they'll force you out of your apartment."

I said, "That could happen."

She offered, "Why don't you live here with me?"

I was stunned, thinking of all the times I'd begged her to live with me. "I thought you didn't want us to live together."

"I didn't want to live together when it meant we would live in the city. But you're welcome to share my cabin."

I felt as mindlessly excited as when I'd first encountered her. We were in Jenny's cabin when she made her offer. I went to embrace her, to thank her, but she held up a warning finger and said, "But don't forget, this is also my place of business, and that has to continue."

Now, pushing open the door, I looked, as always, first at the bed. If a blanket covered our bed sheets, it meant that Jenny had a client booked. It was her way of separating what she called her business bed from our bed, and our own romances in it. There was no blanket and I thought how ironic it was that the people who were bent on destroying us were also likely, if the picketing continued, to alleviate the torment I felt at Jenny's work.

This apart—I mean my discomfort at her work and my tormented waiting—Jenny and I had lived the last few months in a domesticity I'd always longed for, an ephemeral Eden. Through the summer and fall we swam in the early morning. The girls never bothered with clothes and I fell into the same habit. Walking up from the beach with the sea behind us and the huge, deserted woods all around I pictured us as inhabitants of a pristine and innocent world. Then, when I dressed, it was in the cords and boots of the mill workers, bought from the Ratters Lake store, so that I felt, again, a world away from my previous city life.

Now the picketing and the highway construction intruded on, and threatened, our idyll.

One evening when the picketing had been going on for a week, Nurse, the girls and I sat in the dining room. It was seven o' clock and there were no diners, no guests, and no clients for the girls.

"Do you think it's because of the picketers that we have no business?" Nurse asked.

"I don't think so," I told her. "Not just because of the picketers, anyway. They wouldn't stop the guys from the mill. But with the highway already paved half the way from Saint John to St. Stephen, some people are simply travelling through and don't need to break the journey like they used to."

"They still might like to come here to visit us, honey, for the bed and breakfast, even if they don't eat and stay the night," said Megan.

"We don't get the men from the city as much as we used to, though, do we?" said Colleen. "They're all afraid of that Reverend Child and his crowd. That's what one of them told me. Told me that, and that he wouldn't be seeing me again."

Each time we stopped talking, the disciples' chanting and hymn singing pushed into the silence like pain flooding back in after anaesthetic.

Jenny suddenly jumped from her chair beside me and rushed onto the veranda. She screamed in the direction of the highway, "Shut up. Shut up. Shut up."

The chanting stopped. Then we heard applause and laughter and the chanting resumed, louder than before. I led Jenny back inside. She looked around the room and asked, "What will happen to us all?"

After long silence, Nurse said, "We don't know what will happen. Of course we don't. But we do know this: Whatever the future, we'll still have each other, just as we have all these years, you and Megan and Colleen and me. And you have Duncan, too, Jenny. We'll get by. And remember it's not just the Reverend Child and his followers, maddening—frightening, even—though they may be. It's times changing. New roads, new habits, new ways of doing business, including our business. It's not just us being affected by all this. The travellers don't know what's going to happen to them, either, with people buying more and more from the catalogues."

"Maybe we can get our food by catalogues, now Mrs. Eldridge won't serve us," said Colleen.

"No food means no dining room," said Megan.

"The dining room may get closed down anyway," said Nurse. "Duncan, I was going to ask your advice on this. We had a visit yesterday morning from the Health Department. Tell Duncan about it, Megan."

"Well, this guy came to the door with a clipboard in his hand and trying to look important. Said he'd come to inspect the kitchen. Said he suspected it contravened health regulations, whatever they are, and should be closed down. I told him I was on my own and the boss was away and he could come back when Nurse was here. He said he had the right to enter. I told him I had the right to knock his teeth out with my broom—I was sweeping—if he set foot in the house. So he took off, but he said he'd be back, with the police if necessary."

At that moment the *Worley Washes the World* van rattled to a stop beside the veranda steps. Randy, his eyes red, stumbled into the dining room and dropped into a chair. His head fell to his hands and he sobbed. We watched in silence as Nurse went to him, knelt before him, took his hands gently from his face. She eased upwards onto his lap, kissed both his tear strewn cheeks, and pulled his head to her shoulder. As his sobs subsided a little, she whispered, "Tell us what's the matter, Randy."

He raised his head and looked around.

"Sorry, m'darlings. I've been holding that inside me a while, otherwise I couldn't see to drive."

"What's happened?" said Nurse.

Between sobs and indrawn breaths, Randy told us, "Say goodbye to the Count, m' darlings. I just got the news. The guys working on the road told me. He's been killed."

"Dear Count, no," Nurse murmured.

The girls flew together, comforting each other in a tragic triptych. I sat alone, with a vision in my mind of the gentlemanly Count dancing, in his long johns and his homburg, in celebration after the fire.

Randy went on as Nurse stroked his hair, "You know how he never could get used to the train tracks crossing the road. Well, poor old Count, he got ran into by a train at the railroad crossing the other side of St. Stephen. They say it took the train a good while to stop and it dragged the shooting brake along with it. They found the Count, good old Count, by the track, his old homburg, more battered than ever, beside him, his morning coat all ripped to pieces. And there were petticoats and girdles all along the line. They say he kept on blowing his horn right up until the train hit him. I guess he was still trying to warn it to get out of his way."

Later I asked Randy how he'd evaded the picketers. He described the same reception the girls and I received, with the disciples lined up in front of him.

"Then, just when I was going to get out of the van and throw a few of them into the ditch, the boy looks at me, and comes up to the window, and says, 'Sir, you grieve. Forgive our intrusion. May you find solace wherever you can.' And they all fall back. And as I drive through, they all hang their heads, praying, like."

Chapter Eighteen

Mill business took me to Saint John. Nearing the city, I drove out of the woods and along the shore road, where only a stretch of marsh and occasional clumps of tuckamore divided the highway from the sea. As that marine setting gave way, in turn, to the buildings on the outskirts of the town, I reflected on the changes, inner and outer, that circumstances had wrought in me in my shift, like the highway, from urban to rural. It was as if my world had shifted on its axis with my move to Jenny's cabin and to the working world of the mill. As I renounced the city and my legal business, what was left of it after Delap and Ossinger had driven my clients away and foreclosed my rented office, I entered fully the world of the Seashore Boarding House.

I found it a simple world of generally straightforward work at the mill and of evenings at the boarding house, in Jenny's cabin or in the dining room or on the veranda, with the travellers and the woods workers and the girls, with conversations of woods and weather, conversations containing no necessity of impressing anyone. And gradually I discovered in myself a peace and satisfaction with my life that I had never known before. I left a world of striving, to make money, to impress, to influence, and entered one of comradeship and sincerity and openness.

At the same time as I was taking new bearings on my future, adjusting to this shift in my life, I also changed outwardly and obviously. I gave up my business suit, which looked and felt ridiculous in the informal, hard world of the mill, and adopted the dress of the woods workers, cords, heavy shirts, and a wool jacket. My hair was growing longer and was less carefully arranged, without the need to impress clients and judges and colleagues. Now it mattered only that it impressed Jenny, who liked it unkempt. My pale face was even giving way to a swarthier complexion as I spent evenings and weekends on the veranda and on the beach and on the steps of Jenny's cabin.

Most of all I discovered not only a satisfaction and, even, a pride in my new work, simpler and less demanding though it was in many respects compared with my legal practice, but also a new satisfaction and pride in myself and, to my surprise and secret embarrassment, a shame at my old self, to such an extent that I wondered how my friends at the Seashore Boarding House, especially Jenny, had accepted me so readily.

These thoughts drifted through my mind as I drove into the city and parked on King Street in the middle of the business and commercial district I had previously aspired so much to be part of. The first person I saw as I left the car was Theodore Delap. I knew he had seen me, too, because he was hurrying past, looking away, feigning preoccupation. I called to him, knowing how sorely it would embarrass him to be seen in the company of one as disgraced as me, and as shameless, too, to appear in the city centre dressed in my renegade fashion.

"Mr. Delap. How good to see you!"

He was torn between his embarrassment and his inbred veneer of good manners, which prevented him from ignoring me even as it made him recoil from me. He took my arm in his old, patronizing manner, to draw me as far as he could out of the sight of passers by.

"My boy, you're looking—ah—well, considering—ah—considering …"

I shook his hand from my arm, holding my place in the middle of the sidewalk, still smiling my greeting. "Considering my disgrace and my censure at the hands of you and your associates, you mean."

"No, no, my boy, we intended no—ah—censure. We were thinking only of your—ah—your welfare."

"For which I have to thank you, indeed, Mr. Delap. Your concern for my welfare has led me to find a home I love at the Seashore Boarding House and a new job that I enjoy and that truly fulfils me. I am more at peace with myself and with the world than I have been for years. Yes—I thank you."

Unable to draw me aside, he began to edge away from me.

"So good to hear you're doing—ah—well, my boy. But you must excuse me. I have an appointment."

Now I took his arm, as if to lead him, saying, "I didn't mean to detain you. I know how busy you always are. Are you going this way? I'll walk with you."

Together we walked the length of King Street, Delap acknowledging several greetings from colleagues and acquaintances who looked at me curiously and whom I greeted familiarly and boisterously, all the time holding Delap's arm, to pretend our friendship, to Delap's embarrassment.

When we reached the Savoy Grill, on the corner of Germain Street, Delap said, desperately, "I have a luncheon meeting."

"A luncheon meeting? At eleven o' clock in the morning? You must have pressing business to attend to, to start your luncheon so early."

His increasing desperation at my clinging presence made him garrulous and indiscreet.

"Quite so, my boy. Indeed, yes. We have much to attend to. It's the monthly luncheon meeting of the Christian Association of Business and Professional Executives."

"How fortunate! I'll accompany you. I am still a member, am I not, with my fees paid until the end of the year? And I don't believe I was ever actually expelled from the Association, was I?"

I steered him unwillingly into the Savoy, with the intention of further embarrassing him and his friends—my former colleagues—with my insouciant presence and my denial of their efforts to belittle and destroy me. But once inside, seeing again their old suited self-importance, their self-conscious posturing, I recoiled, tired of my game and fearing my incipient anger would overrun me.

"You disgust me, all of you," I said quietly, and left.

I sauntered the length of Germain Street and turned onto Water Street, enjoying my own self-consciousness of my rebel status, fancying myself the lone iconoclast amongst all the preening self importance of the city. Water Street ran parallel to the harbour and I loved to look down the narrow streets running from it to the water, where ships loomed, sudden and huge, dwarfing the row houses, throwing perspective askew. I strolled down narrow Wharf Lane to the waterfront.

This was the oldest part of the city, a labyrinth of narrow streets which was constantly threatened by redevelopment. Women on the steps of corner stores, headscarves bobbing under the fading signs on the brickwork above the shop windows—*Bigelow's Jams—Very Tasty, Wheaton's Breads—Always Fresh, Katy's Kitchen on the Korner—All Your Teatime Needs*. Men in little groups, sharing a newspaper. Children playing in the gutter and on the steps between the wrought iron railings leading up to the once imposing doorways. In the harbour, the small fishing fleet looked out of place mingling with the tankers and cargo ships from Europe and South America. I wondered how long it would be before it became a quaint thing of the past. The fleet was like my friends, I reflected, the ragged believers of the Seashore Boarding House, anachronistic, bohemian relics struggling for survival among the crushing forces of a new age.

I left the harbour by Horsefield Lane, where many of the houses, with vacancies created by the diaspora of the prostitutes, still displayed *Apartment for Rent* signs. A lace curtain in a window on the other side of the road moved and a woman, hair like frayed rope, cigarette dangling from her lips, dressed only in a slip with one shoulder strap hanging, moved across the window, paused, looked at me before disappearing. I wondered where and how Maud and Mandy were selling their tricks, whether they had been driven to deliver them clandestinely, like the woman in the window, or whether they had found a market place as cheerfully promiscuous and honest as Horsefield Lane had once been.

I walked back to Water Street, to the offices of the mill's customs agents, where I completed my business regarding a new contract for supplying lumber across the border. Then, with time on my hands while our agents drew up papers for me to sign, I walked back to *Katy's Kitchen*.

The cafe was quiet after the lunchtime rush of warehousemen, longshoremen and seamen. It was the first time I'd been there since moving out to the boarding house. Katy looked up and nodded briefly when I walked in, then looked again and, recognizing me, came out from behind her counter and hugged me. She stood back, hands on my shoulders, and said, "Well, look at you now."

While I sat at the counter with a plate of her homemade baked beans, she pulled a postcard from the wall behind the counter and passed it to me without comment. I read:

Hi Katy. We made it up to Trois Rivieres, over the Quebec border. Mandy is coughing badly after we spent three nights on the road wet and cold and sleeping in ditches before we got a ride. She always was the delicate one, not like me, older but tougher. We have a room here but money is short, it being difficult for me to do business with Mandy coughing in the other bed. Remember us to the guys. Fond memories—Maud.

"I wish I could have helped them more," I said.

"You did plenty. If it wasn't for you, they'd be in jail now, with all the other girls the police picked up around that time."

"Mandy might have been healthier in jail."

"Yes—and unhappier, too. What would you rather be, free and sick, or locked up and healthy?"

"I've never thought about it."

"Oh, yes, you have. I know what they did to you, your business so-called friends, and I know where you are now. You could have done what they wanted and you'd be here in the city now, strutting around in your suit like you used to, full of your own importance, and miserable. But you stuck to what you believed in and, boy, you're looking good on it. Here, the tea's on me."

The door of the café opened and Katy greeted the new customer with, "Another renegade. What'll it be today, doc? The usual?"

While he ordered I studied him covertly. Short, bald and bespectacled, he couldn't have looked less like a renegade. I realized he was studying me, too, looking, like me, for signs of the renegade status Katy had accorded us. I caught his eye and nodded, acknowledging our strange affinity.

Katy leaned on the counter, close to the newcomer, and said, conspiratorially, "This kind gentleman helped two of our girls elude the police."

Katy's customer inclined his head in my direction.

"What makes you one of Katy's renegades?" I asked.

"I'll tell you what he did," said Katy. "He defied the hospital board, that's what. When the ladies and the gentlemen of the board decided their contribution to cleaning up the city, as they called it, was that the hospital wouldn't allow any of our girls in for treatment there, not for anything, colds, flu, stomach upsets, nothing, Dr. Michaud here, he organized the protest by the staff. And they told the hospital board they didn't care what they said, they'd keep on looking after the girls, just like they looked after everyone who came to the hospital. And in the end, the board backed off. Right, doc?"

"They did, but it wasn't a pretty fight, with that church dominating the board, and then the Association of Business and Professional Executives joining in, and some of our own staff members of it."

While Katy went into the kitchen to prepare Dr. Michaud's meal, we fell into conversation about the hospital. I couldn't help asking him whether he knew a Dr. Noel Gallant.

"Do you know Noel?" Dr. Michaud asked.

"He's an old friend of an old friend."

"Poor Noel had a hard time of it. This would be some fifteen years ago. His wife had always been a clinging sort, but then suddenly she changed. Some inexplicable resentment surfaced and her clinging turned into contempt for him, and for his efforts to keep her happy. In the end she left him and went out west. He carried on here for a couple of years but he was miserable and lost, the poor man. Then he went up north to work. We exchanged a few letters but I lost touch with him."

Driving out of the city, I pondered on the idiosyncrasies and eccentricities of love, on how the love between Nurse and Noel Gallant had brought only lasting sorrow to three lives, to Nurse (I thought of her crying when she spoke of him, even after all these years), and to her doctor lover, and to his wife; and on how my love for Jenny (I couldn't, alas, say her love for me) had brought its share of joy, but a joy often tempered with misery. As the shore road gave way to the woods, I thought: But I would not exchange those tortured evenings of waiting on the beach, those fallings out over her work, my chagrin at her refusal to speak of love, I would not exchange all those for a more comfortable, but lesser, love with a more conventional lover.

Chapter Nineteen

It was forest fire season again, and a bad one, in the spring of 1938. So many fires were burning that it seemed as if the whole province was aflame. Only those fires threatening communities received attention. The rest were left to burn out of control or until they burned themselves out when they reached the coast, so that they raged alone in the wilderness like children venting tantrums in an empty room. At the boarding house we breathed smoke, and a fine layer of ash covered everything. The girls swept the dining room several times a day to keep the ash from accumulating. The sun was a red omen behind the smoke, adding to the atmosphere of menace, and the wind became something to be raged at for its incessant kindling and fanning of the fires.

It blew from the west, treacherously benevolent in its balmy warmth. When a lightning strike started a small fire on the edge of St. Stephen, the fire crews paid it scant heed. Then, as the wind carried it away from the town, they turned their attention elsewhere, leaving it to burn into the huge uninhabited area to the east of the town. If the wind held, it would burn well to the north of Saint John and then into the deserted interior of the province. Only the small communities in the woods lay in its path.

And the Seashore Boarding House.

"Trouble, threat," said Charlie, as soon as he heard of the fire.

For the tabernacle, the fire was like a manifestation of its power and the disciples exulted in it. On the radio they prayed their thanks for the scourging of the province and when they realized the Seashore Boarding House was in the path of the fire they rejoiced.

To the applause of the congregation, the Reverend Child announced in his Sunday morning sermon that they would end their picketing of the

Seashore Boarding House and that he would visit the establishment himself before the fire destroyed it and would attempt to bring the joy of atonement to its inhabitants.

"We have stood at the gates of this Sodom and begged its owner and its inhabitants and its clients to forsake their sin," he declared. "Now let us carry the fight into hell itself. I will be your Daniel in the lions' den and I will turn their will for evil into submission to the way of the Lord. Tomorrow evening I will go alone and I will bring them to our purifying fire of salvation."

I heard the news of this latest crusade the next morning from a docker who'd come out from Saint John looking for work at the mill. As soon as I could, I hurried back to the boarding house to warn Nurse.

She was on the veranda watching the smoke from the fire roiling upwards in the west. The front of the fire was only a few miles away. As soon as the smoke died down in one place, it erupted in another as the flames moved on to fresh fodder. The wind roared relentlessly.

Nurse greeted me with, "Are we going to be burned out?"

"Maybe. It looks as if Messalonskee will be gone by the end of today unless the wind shifts direction, and it hasn't done that for weeks. The villagers are getting out now. We sent a couple of trucks to help them."

"And after Messalonskee?"

"Eagle Rock will be burned. Then Ratters Lake. The villagers there are already packed and loaded and ready to get out. The guys have taken trucks there, too."

"Should we get ready to run?"

I'd been wondering when to tell Nurse what Charlie had told me that morning. "If the fire continues to burn like it is now, Charlie says you and the girls should be ready tomorrow. He says the fire may come through here, or it may just miss the boarding house. If it burns like it is now, on its present course, we'll be on the edge. I'll send a truck out early tomorrow, just in case. But don't despair yet. It could still miss us."

145

As I spoke, the wind teasingly diminished, then resumed with even greater ferocity, as if to mock my reassurance. Beyond the meadow, the waves fought to break on the shore as the gale, roaring along the coast, dragged the surf parallel to the shore, whipping foam from the peaks of the waves before they threw themselves on the beach.

The Bear Pots clattered furiously and incessantly.

Nurse's gaze travelled between the spiraling smoke and the raging surf.

Recalling the reason for my early return to the boarding house, I said, "I've just heard some news of our friends, the disciples. They've ended their picketing …"

"I noticed they'd gone."

"… And the Reverend Child is going to pay us a visit. He's going to convert us—you, in particular."

Nurse said, "Is he, indeed?"

She paced to the end of the veranda. She watched the distant smoke, which had settled in one area and was now billowing upward in another. It was as if her thoughts were racing from one threat to the other.

She asked, "Is he coming alone?"

"That was his boast, so I think that's what he'll do."

"This evening?"

"That's what he said."

Nurse turned to me. Her hair swirled furiously around her face as she turned her back to the wind. Her eyes were shot with tears. I didn't know whether they were provoked by her gazing into the wind, or by rage at Pastor Oagles and his followers, or by sorrow at the prospect of loss.

"Fetch the girls," she instructed. "And get Charlie—can you? We have to plan how we'll receive the Reverend Child."

"Shall we talk to him? Try and reason with him?"

"No. Oh, no."

"What then?"

"We'll seduce him."

We gathered in the dining room late in the afternoon to receive our instructions. Charlie and I were to hide in the kitchen and be witness to everything that happened.

"You are a lawyer. People will believe you," she told me. "And you, dear Charlie, you are old and respectable and in mill management. People will believe you, too."

The girls were to wait in their cabins until the Reverend Child arrived and were to appear fifteen minutes later, looking their most beguiling. Nurse, meanwhile, would await our visitor.

He arrived at five o' clock, business suited and briefcase in hand. Charlie and I peered through the crack in the kitchen door as he mounted the veranda steps. As I watched I was struck again by the feeling of having met the Reverend Child somewhere before that day I picked him up outside Saint John.

In her white uniform and red sash, Nurse answered the door. "Reverend Child. Welcome to the Seashore Boarding House."

He inclined his head in a little bow. "Madam."

"Is this a business visit or are you here for social reasons?"

"I come on business. I would have no other reason for visiting."

"Does your business allow you to enter or would you consider that socializing?"

"I will enter, if invited."

Nurse stepped back and extended her arm. "Do come in. Can I offer you some tea?"

"Thank you, madam, but the Lord's work prohibits the indulgence of appetites."

"Do you never indulge your appetites, Reverend Child?"

"The Lord gave us our appetites in order to test our moral resolve, not to provide a means of easy pleasure."

"I had never considered the taking of tea to be so morally reprehensible. Is sitting down also considered indulging one's appetite?"

"You mock me."

"Of course. But do sit down, anyway."

Nurse indicated two chairs across the room and near the kitchen door. We had placed them there in preparation for the Reverend Child's visit so that Charlie and I had a clear view of everything that happened. The Reverend Child sat with his briefcase on his knees.

Nurse sat facing him and asked, "Now, how can I help you?"

"Madam," he began, "you offend our beliefs and that distresses my congregation."

"I am sorry for that," Nurse countered. "But I have my own beliefs, which sustain me, and are free of reproach, at least in my mind."

"But you offend my Lord."

"I may offend your Lord but I do not offend mine."

"Do we not all have the same Lord?"

"I suspect not."

"But there is only one."

"Then that is the one I do not offend."

The Reverend Child, who had leaned forward as he spoke, placing his briefcase beside him on the floor, leaned back, paused, and started again. "I know this is a place of sin."

Nurse crossed her legs, folded her arms, considered. "It is a place of friendship, love and comfort. Is that sin?"

"When love and comfort are lust and debauchery, yes, that is sin. I beg you to renounce this evil and to embrace the wholesome, Christian way of life we espouse. Let me conduct you through the ceremony of the purification by fire. Become one of us."

"We have experienced Pastor Oagles's attempts to purify us by fire."

The Reverend Child waved a dismissive, contemptuous hand. "Pastor Oagles sometimes acted precipitously in his zeal, for which you must forgive him, as we forgive them that trespass against us."

Nurse leaned forward abruptly and as she spoke, the Reverend Child's eyes lighted hopefully. "Suppose I accept the purification by fire and renounce my business, what will become of the Seashore Boarding House, if it survives the fire? It has been my home for some twenty years and has housed my family, not a family in your narrow sense but a family nevertheless, because we care for each other. What will become of the boarding house? What will become of us?"

"You mean what will become of these loggers and woods workers and travellers? What did Pastor Oagles call them—a bunch of ragged believers? They can dine and satisfy themselves at home in far healthier manner than they can at the Seashore Boarding House. And what will become of you— you and your girls? I have a plan for all that." He reached down and tapped his briefcase. "A business plan! We, the Tabernacle of the Disciples of Fire, plan to open a Christian retreat, where disciples and neophytes and their families can gather in fellowship and worship."

"And the Seashore Boarding House …?"

"Yes. The Seashore Boarding House is ideally situated, between, but away from, the town of St. Stephen and the city of Saint John. It would become that retreat. And you, with your organizational and management skills, not to mention your medical knowledge, would run it, with your staff as assistants."

"You would have the madam of a brothel run your Christian retreat?"

"The *former* madam, yes."

"And of course you would relish the publicity that would generate."

He smiled and nodded. "What a coup for the Tabernacle of the Disciples of Fire."

Nurse seemed to contemplate. "And we would have to undergo this purification by fire?"

He waved his hand dismissively again. "A publicity stunt. It looks impressive but means nothing. It doesn't hurt—unless you want it to, of course." He held up his scarred hands and went on, "When thou walkest through the fire, thou shalt not be burned; neither shall the fire kindle upon thee. Actually, the fire burns in a closely controlled U shape. Your hands are placed between the arms of the U, only warming them slightly, if you don't leave them there too long."

He leaned forward earnestly, pulling his chair forward so that he confronted Nurse more closely.

"The real redemption is in the cry from your heart for forgiveness. For this ye know, that no whoremonger, nor unclean person, hath any inheritance in the kingdom of God. The public display may be a stunt but the heart cry must be sincere and real. If it is not, our Lord will know and will not accept your appeal. Then, indeed, if you try to deceive Him, the fire shall take you. It is written, I will remind you, that if she profane herself by playing the whore, she shall be burnt with fire."

Fifteen minutes exactly had passed since his arrival and right on cue we heard footsteps on the veranda. Jenny, Colleen and Megan entered.

"Ah, my colleagues," said Nurse. "I thought it important that they, too, hear what you have to say."

The girls had been instructed to appear at their most seductive and they had excelled themselves. Jenny, like the others, was dressed in white. She wore a long, loose dress which, I realized with a gasp of admiration as it swirled around her as she moved, was slit on both sides, exposing to the thigh those familiar legs. The fresh sea salt smell the girls always carried with them pervaded the room and reached into the kitchen. Charlie looked at me, raised his eyebrows and licked his lips. I wondered whether the Reverend Child's reaction was the same.

Nurse rose and stood beside the girls.

"This is Megan ..."

Megan curtsied. The Reverend Child stood uncertainly.

"And Colleen …"

Colleen also curtsied.

"And Jenny."

Jenny in her turn curtsied. As the girls bobbed they leaned forwards so that the front of their dresses fell open, offering the Reverend Child a glimpse of bosom.

Nurse told him, "Please be seated."

He sat. He clasped his hands. Unclasped them and wiped them on his knees. Clasped them before him again.

Nurse turned to the girls. "This gentleman would like to address you. Please give your full attention to what he has to say and consider it carefully. It concerns the future of the Seashore Boarding House and the future of all of us."

The girls immediately grouped themselves around him, as if anxious to listen intently to his message. Megan sat on one side, pulling her chair so close that her knee brushed his, and Colleen, sitting on the other side, had her face only inches from his ear, so that each time she breathed out, she breathed warm air into his ear. Twice he turned to her to prevent it, but the sight of her tongue lolling lasciviously between her teeth was enough to make him turn his ear to her again. Jenny sat at his feet, facing him, her bosom visible as her dress fell forwards, and her legs drawn up, innocently exposing the backs of her thighs.

The girls gazed expectantly at the Reverend Child, waiting for him to speak. Twice he opened his mouth and twice nothing happened. His eyes, searching desperately for safe landing, touched on the flickering tongue, the creamy bosoms, the exposed thighs, before they came to rest on Nurse.

"Go ahead, sir," she said.

He started, "You have all sinned."

Colleen nodded happily.

"But that is not cause for despair. It is cause for hope. Think of the joy of redemption …"

"Say that again," Jenny interrupted.

The Reverend Child stopped, blinked, looked down at her, dragged his eyes upwards again as she moved slightly, letting her dress expose one leg to the hip.

He began again.

"You have all sinned, but …"

"No. Not that part—just the last bit," she said.

"Think of …"

"Say 'think' again."

Jenny was looking closely at his face, kneeling up. This was the part of the plot where Nurse had told the girls they would have to improvise and Jenny was obviously taking the lead.

Confused, the Reverend Child repeated, "Think …"

Megan was now staring intently into his face.

"Nurse, quick, take a look at this," she said. "Say 'think' again, honey."

"What is this?" the Reverend Child started but Jenny interrupted again.

"Just say 'think,'" she demanded.

Nurse, who had been standing to one side, joined the girls in front of him.

"Think," he said.

"Put out your tongue," said Nurse.

"Why?"

"I am trained as a nurse. Do not question me. Just do as I say."

The Reverend Child extended his tongue. Nurse examined it.

"Hmmm. I feared as much. Thank you, girls, for corroborating what I already half suspected as soon as our guest started to talk. Reverend Child, you must take all your weight off your feet immediately. Lie on the floor, please."

"I will not."

"You are concerned in your work with the saving of souls from sin. Very well. I am concerned in much of my work, as you know, with the saving of people from ill health and even death. Now you, sir, are in poor health right now and could die at any moment unless you consent to follow my advice. Your tongue is an unhealthy red and where it is not red it is tinged with blue. You are highly excitable and your breathing, I have noticed since you came in, is shallow and rapid. In short, you have all the signs of acute pulmonary peristalsis and you could fall into a coma at any moment. You must allow me to do what I am trained to do. Take the weight completely from your feet and alleviate some of the stress on your heart. Now—lie down!"

The Reverend Child lay on the floor.

"Loosen his necktie, Colleen. And Megan, expose his chest so that I can listen to his heart. Jenny, cushion the gentleman's head."

The Reverend Child found his head laid against Jenny's bare inner thigh, while gentle, expert hands loosened his collar and unbuttoned his shirt.

"I'm perfectly all right," he managed to say, before Jenny's head bent low over his face, her lips brushing his cheek, and she murmured, "Don't worry. Relax. We'll take care of you."

Nurse produced a stethoscope and, kneeling beside him, applied it to his chest. She muttered, "Hmmm," and said, feeling his belt, "This is restricting the flow of blood. Loosen it, girls."

She stood back to watch.

Who could resist? Certainly not the young, celibate Reverend Child who, like Pastor Oagles, sheathed his rampant lust in sanctimonious self-denial, at once fearing his desire and craving its satisfaction.

Charlie and I watched enviously as he lay back and submitted to the expert, professional attentions of the girls of the Seashore Boarding House.

"Now breathing really shallow, respiration actually rapid," Charlie whispered, as the Reverend Child lay limp under their undressing, caressing hands. Limp except for the one part of his body which, when it was finally exposed, caused even those experienced girls to pause and gaze.

"Penis rufus," Nurse gasped. "I've seen it only once before and they say you encounter only one case in a lifetime. Only one ..."

She had gone quite white and seemed mesmerised by the scarlet tumescence.

"Leave this to me, girls," she said. "I will deal with this gentleman myself."

Jenny, Megan and Colleen fell back, leaving the Reverend Child sprawled on the floor, vulnerable in his near nakedness.

Nurse said, "Out!"

The girls, looking at one another in bewilderment, retreated outside, while Charlie and I continued our secret witness, wondering why Nurse had changed her plan. The girls were to have seduced the Reverend Child, at which point Charlie and I would appear as witnesses ready to blackmail him into abandoning his campaign against the Seashore Boarding House.

Nurse sat. She wrapped her arms around herself, as if hugging herself, and rocked in her chair.

"Get up," she ordered. "Get dressed."

The Reverend Child obeyed, watching Nurse for some new trickery. Just before he refastened his trousers she beckoned him to her. She reached peremptorily into his underwear and again exposed the shrinking, crimson organ.

"Have you had this all your life?" she demanded.

He gasped as she still gripped him. "Of course."

"I mean the colour of it. Has it always been this way?"

"As long as I can remember. Will you mock me with it?"

"Of course not. I am a nurse. I do not mock the aberrations of the body."

"Then please preserve me some modesty."

"You have no modesty before me."

"I had when I arrived, before you set about corrupting me."

"I say you have none before me. A child's nakedness is no loss of modesty."

"I am not a child."

Nurse released his shrunken organ. She studied him for a long time, hugging herself and rocking in her chair again. She murmured, "It struck me as soon as I saw you. You were so familiar. Somehow—I knew you. But I could not believe it, especially when you were the one trying to destroy me."

Even before she spoke again, I knew what she would say, suddenly understanding the strange familiarity which made me think I had met him before, suddenly remembering what she had told me years before.

"You are my child."

His assurance and arrogance had returned with his dress. He held his hands towards her as if warding her off. "Scheming Jezebel. Will you mock me further?"

"You are my son."

"You are a whore and you dare to pretend I am your son."

"You are my son—and you seek to destroy your mother!"

"Scheming sinner. How would I be your son?"

Nurse pointed between his legs. He covered himself there.

"You have the mark my son had, the red blemished penis, one of the rarest aberrations of nature. It marks you as one among millions. I caressed it. I pitied it. I saw its first tiny erection eighteen years ago as I nursed you, too briefly. You are my son!"

"I came here on behalf of my Lord to beg you to renounce the evil business of this place and to offer you a new, Christian way of life. Your response is first to seek to disgrace me and ridicule me, then to shame me as the child of a whore. I thought Pastor Oagles was mad in his viciousness toward you but now I see that he was right. The Lord's fire should destroy you."

"You threaten your mother?"

"I call on the fire of my Lord to smite a scheming whore."

"You are my son! I had to give you up for adoption because I was young and unmarried and I could not care for you."

"So now you accuse me of being the unwanted product of some casual, illicit copulation."

Nurse fell to her knees and, clasping her hands together, held them to him as if in prayer. "I accuse you of nothing except a failure to recognize your own mother, who kneels before you now begging you to forgive her for giving you away. Please understand. I had no choice. I was barely able to care for myself, let alone a baby. Please, my son, recognize me. Believe me. I am your mother."

From somewhere near the shore we heard shouted warnings. At the same time the Bear Pots began to clang an ever more furious alarm and I realized that the wind had intensified and was roaring from the west like a huge, unrelenting bellows. I made out the cries at the same time as Nurse and the Reverend Child heard them: "The fire is coming! The fire is coming!"

The Reverend Child, looking out of the window, cried triumphantly, "And there went out fire from the Lord."

The smoke reached us first, pouring through the open door and windows into the dining room in a rolling, roiling mass. Charlie and I retreated out of the back door, shouting to Nurse and the Reverend Child to follow. When they didn't appear, we tried to re-enter but were driven back by the dense cloud filling the house and now pouring out of the back door. We crawled under the smoke around to the front to try and enter with the wind and smoke at our backs. We made it to the veranda steps. We scrambled up them and crawled to the door. There, for a second, the smoke parted. On the far side of the dining room we saw them. The Reverend

Child faced us. His arms were held out as if to embrace the smoke. He chanted words only some of which I caught before they were snatched away by the wind: "The Lord my God is a consuming fire … A passionate fire … An avenging fire … A triumphant fire …"

Behind him Nurse was on her knees, her gaze fixed on her son, her hands held up to him like a supplicant beseeching a harsh god.

I shouted, "Nurse, Child, get out. Crawl. This way."

Then thick smoke swirled around them again, obscuring them. Gasping for air, we were forced back again.

Now came the fire itself, skipping through the tops of the trees in a sinuous, evil dance. At the edge of the clearing in which the boarding house stood it paused, like a predatory animal contemplating its next victim. For a few seconds, in my naïveté at the power of a forest fire, I thought the clearing would hold it. Then, suddenly, flames were in the tops of the trees behind the boarding house, and on the other side of the clearing, and on the roof. Charlie and I staggered down the veranda steps as the smoke, having filled the house, poured back out of the door onto the veranda. As we stepped from the veranda, the fire crew from the mill arrived.

Lamarre jumped from the truck, gasping, "The mill's gone. We had to run. Thought we might save the boarding house."

"Nurse, inside," Charlie shouted, pointing to the door.

Lamarre and Sonny threw themselves up the steps and through the door but were driven back, choking. While Sonny coughed on all fours, Lamarre tried again, and again staggered out, retching, eyes streaming. The men pulled him clear. He forced them off. Struggled to his feet. Set off toward the house again. This time Sonny, still on his knees, grabbed him and held him, hugging him.

It was no longer air that we breathed but heat and smoke.

Charlie gasped, "Give up. Hopeless. Make for beach, head for water. Fast. Quick. Meadow burning, grass afire."

We ran, Charlie and I, the mill fire crew, Sonny and Lamarre supporting each other like wounded soldiers, across the meadow toward the beach,
where we could see the girls, white figures shimmering through the waves
of heat rising from the meadow. We danced over the flames that rose and
fell like waves through the grass. A moose, head up and antlers back,
charged out of the burning trees and passed us, eyes wide and blind in
terror. Three deer ran wildly along the beach, their hooves skittering on
the weed covered shingle. A bear lurched out of the woods behind the
boarding house. For a delirious moment I wondered whether he might be
the originator of the still sounding Bear Pots, still looking for his scraps of
curing after all these years.

From the beach we watched the Seashore Boarding House burn, while
fire raged through the woods around and no rescuing waves came this
time. It seemed as if the fire was gone in minutes, leaving the meadow a
patchwork of green, grey and black, the forest a smoking tangle of blackened trunks and smouldering brush, where flames suddenly flickered up
out of the ground and as abruptly died back down. We breathed the smell
of ash instead of fire and smoke.

The girls had been standing in the shallows, splashing water onto their
dresses for fear of their catching fire with the burning embers blowing
from the trees. Now they came slowly forward, holding on to one another.
Charlie, Lamarre and Sonny stood with heads bowed and hands clasped
before them, as if in prayer. I held my hand out to Jenny but her arms were
clasped around Megan and Colleen and she would not let go. The wind
had died with the passing of the fire and now no breath of even a breeze
disturbed the trees that had survived. The sea, rather than raging in response to the ferocity of the wind and the fire, seemed to have been stilled
by it, so that the tiny waves it threw up broke in silent ripples. No birds
sang in their usual clamour around the clearing.

Charlie said, "Reckon go look. Guess must see."

We picked our way silently through the meadow, through patches of unscathed grass that shone an insolent green against the areas of burn and ash. As we stood uncertainly before the boarding house, surveying the broken windows, the still burning roof, the flames licking from two upstairs windows, Randy's van roared in from the highway. He jumped out and ran to us, calling, "I couldn't get through to help, m'darlings. Are you safe? Is anyone hurt?"

I said, "Nurse … Inside … We don't know …"

Charlie climbed slowly, reluctantly, onto the veranda. He looked back at us once, then crossed to the door. He peered into the dining room. He looked back again and said, "Please—help me. I beg—assist me."

A lick of flame surged through and along the veranda as fire caught grass and debris beneath it. Charlie stepped back to avoid it. The flames died down again, except at the end of the veranda, where they burned steadily on the rails and up the wall.

We mounted the steps, stamping on the persistent flames. Charlie led us inside.

The fire had enjoyed the old timbered house. The wall between the dining room and the kitchen was gone, Nurse's counter and office with it. The upstairs floor tilted dangerously and where the floor had burned through I could see into one of the guest rooms, the one in which I'd stayed on my first night at the Seashore Boarding House. My restless bed of that night was a bare, blackened frame, and the jug and bowl lay broken on the floor. Most of the dining room tables and chairs had been easy fodder for the fire, as had the old pine boards of the floor. But it had danced an ironic circle around Nurse and her son, who lay apparently unscathed, but unmoving. We could find no sign of a pulse, no sign of breathing, in either.

Nurse had her arms wrapped around her son's knees, and he lay turned away from her.

Chapter Twenty

Jenny said, "We're going to move on, Megan and Colleen and me."

I said stupidly, knowing the answer, "What will you do?"

"What we do—used to do—here at the boarding house. What earns us a living."

We were on the beach. The girls were on the rocks, in their white dresses. I sat nearby on my old, familiar, waiting rock. It was the evening before Nurse's funeral. I looked across at Jenny. She was biting her lip, frowning.

Megan and Colleen smiled sadly, looking from Jenny to me.

Jenny rose, climbed from the rock, and walked slowly to me. I fixed my eyes on the horizon where the sun was about to drop behind the islands of Pocomoonshine Bay. I could not bear to see her resoluteness. She sat beside me and leaned her head on my shoulder. I put my arm around her.

"Where will you go?"

"Across the border somewhere. We'll go down to Bangor first and try our luck there."

"And it's useless for me to ask you to stay?"

She murmured, "Yes," then added quickly, "Please don't think too badly of me."

"Why—how—would I ever think badly of you?"

"For leaving you like this. For sticking with the girls instead of with you."

"You and Megan and Colleen were together for a long time before I came along. I know you all need one other more than you need me."

"You were ready for this, weren't you?"

"I've always been ready for your leaving me. I was always half expecting—and half afraid—that one day you'd tell me something like this."

"Sorry."

"There's nothing to be sorry for."

Pocomoonshine Bay was already in shadow. The tide was low and the seals had abandoned their rock for the day. We watched the sun dip below the islands. For a few moments it lingered among the tops of the trees in the fire ravaged woods around us and glinted on the tin roof of the doomed Seashore Boarding House. Then they, too, fell into shadow.

Megan said, shaking her head, "You two."

Colleen said, "Go on, Jenny. Tell him. Tell him you love him. You know you do."

Jenny pushed her head into my shoulder. My neck was wet with her tears.

Chapter Twenty-One

Nurse's funeral was held at the little Ratters Lake Church, where the ragged believers of the Seashore Boarding House, the girls and the travellers, the mill workers and the woods workers, gathered, as well as many of Nurse's patients from the woods communities. The girls had decided I should speak the eulogy.

I talked about Nurse's devotion and skill as a nurse during the twenty years she had lived in the woods. I went on, "More than this, and needing no acknowledgement from me because it is so well known, is the gratitude owed to her by the people of the woods communities, here in Ratters Lake, as well as Hedgehog Mountain, Eagle Rock, Messalonskee, Goose Cove and Nepisguit. You do not need me to express what we owe to Nurse for her selfless work all these years. I know you have amply expressed it to her over the years, in different ways. I do want to suggest, however, what the sum of all our gratitude should be: That if saints can exist in modern times, then she was—she is—a saint. Nurse is the Saint of the Woods, the Saint of the Seashore Boarding House."

As I left the lectern and sat down, Randy Fudge rose and spoke from his pew. "There's another side of Nurse—that's the only name we ever knew her by, although she was never a nurse, as such, to me—there's another side of Nurse, m'darlings, some of us here knew, that all of you should know."

I looked up at the huge, bulky figure, wondering what he was going to say, but I should have remembered he was a salesman, not lacking in diplomacy. He winked at me before continuing.

"That other side was one of a warmth and friendship which lit the countryside between Saint John and St. Stephen. Would you, I wonder, be wanting to travel this route often, like my friends and me do? There's nothing on the road, m'darlings—nothing for the eighty miles between the towns except trees, and dust, and rocks, and flies, and bog ... and the Seashore Boarding House. I'm proud to say I was one of the first guests to stay there, one of the first to experience what we travellers appreciate more than most, a warmth and a welcome which went beyond what you'd expect from a roadside stopping place. Us travellers, like the late, dear old, good old Count and me, we looked forward to stopping at the Seashore Boarding House, with Nurse and the girls, and were proud to be counted as part of its family. I'd say it was a home away from home, except that most of us travellers don't really have a home, just a succession of places to stay in for a night or two, including what we call our own places. So I think, for all of us, the Seashore Boarding House, with the special warmth that Nurse created there, became our home, and Nurse and her girls, and the other regulars there, became our family.

"So will you be remembering, m'darlings, what we travellers will remember of her, and give your thanks for what we give our thanks for—her kindness, her nursing skill, her generosity, her warmth, her love. I don't know who I've lost—a sister, a mother, a friend ..."

Randy's voice faltered and died away, and he stood uncertainly. Colleen took his arm, drew him down into his pew, and as he wept, wept with him, with a comforting arm around the broad, shaking shoulders.

The short journey through the woods to the Ratters Lake cemetery looked more like a carnival procession than a funeral cortege. I filled my car with Nurse's more elderly patients, while Charlie and Mrs. Charlie followed in the truck, the girls in the open back, in their white dresses. They were like beauty queens on parade. Following them came Randy's gaudy van, then the logging trucks, the trucks of the mill workers, and the horse drawn wagons of the villagers.

The girls' thin dresses waved and fluttered in the wind, so that looking back as we drove I saw the old truck with angel wings trying to lift it from the dusty woods road.

Visit us at www.speakingvolumes.us

www.ingramcontent.com/pod-product-compliance
Lightning Source LLC
Chambersburg PA
CBHW020640250626
47154CB00008B/2752